FORGET THE ALAMO!

Book 1 of the Lone Star Reloaded Series

A tale of alternative history

By Drew McGunn

All rights reserved.

ISBN: 1977848842
ISBN-13: 978-1977848840

This book is a work of fiction. Names, characters, places and incidents are the product of the author's overactive imagination or are used fictitiously. Any resemblance to actual events, or locales is coincidental. Fictional characters are entirely fictional and any resemblance among the fictional characters to any person living or dead is coincidental. Historical figures in the book are portrayed on a fictional basis and any actions or inactions on their part that diverge from actual history are for story purposes only.

Copyright © 2017 by Drew McGunn

All Rights Reserved. No part of this this publication may be reproduced, stored in a retrieval system or transmitted, in any form or by any means, electronic, mechanical, photocopying, recordings, or otherwise, without the prior permission of the publisher and copyright holder. Permission may be sought by contacting the author at drewmcgunn@gmail.com

The image of the Alamo on the cover is © 2006 Larry D. Moore. See Licensing below.

Attribution Specification: For any reuse or distribution of this image, please attribute with at least the photographer's name Larry D. Moore along with the license information in a format of your choosing.

Example: Larry D. Moore CC BY-SA 3.0.

https://commons.wikimedia.org/wiki/File:Alamo_replica.jpg

Newsletter Sign Up/Website address:
https://drewmcgunn.wixsite.com/website

V1

FORGET THE ALAMO!

TABLE OF CONTENTS

Chapter 1

The sandstorm's last gust of wind shook the HMMWV in which Staff Sergeant Will Travers rode shotgun. He chuckled as he considered how much the military loved acronyms. Calling it a High Mobility Multipurpose Wheeled Vehicle took too long. Like millions of soldiers before him, to Will it was just a Humvee. Dust filtered into the vehicle, coating him and his driver, Sergeant Edgar Smith. He brushed away a light coating from his jacket sleeves, exposing a divisional T-patch insignia on his left shoulder. Will tried looking out the passenger side window and saw that it was caked in dust. He rolled it down, then back up, creating streaks that allowed him to see the arid countryside as the tactical vehicle rolled along the sand covered road.

The current mission, like most others, was convoy duty; escorting supplies from Baghdad to one of the many bases around central Iraq. As he looked out the dirty window, Will counted down the days until he would return to Texas and go back to two days a month and two weeks during the summer. The Texas Army National Guard's 36th Infantry Division was nearing the end of a nine-month rotation in Iraq and when he thought about it, he was thoroughly sick of the dry, oppressive heat and ever-present sand. He missed his parents and friends and longed to be back in his hometown, Galveston.

"Hey, Will, did you get your voter's registration filled out? You know, the deadline to register to vote is next week for November, right?" Sergeant Edgar Smith said, speaking over the roar of the Humvee's engine.

Will peeled his eyes away from the monotonous desertscape sliding by the window, and said, "Yeah. My folks sent me the mail-in ballot along with a bunch of McCain bumper stickers. You figure out who you're gonna vote for, Smitty?"

Keeping both hands on the steering wheel, he shrugged his shoulders and replied, "Either way, my vote's not gonna count. Texas ain't gonna vote for a black man, am I right or what?"

Will corrected him, "That's half-black. You know, like the duck from the insurance ad."

Smith laughed and said, "Best not let First Sergeant Washington hear you say that. To hear him talk, Obama's the second coming of Jesus."

Will shook his head, "All those politicians are the same. The only reason that I'd consider voting for McCain is that when he's lying, at least he's telling me what I want to hear. Most of the time, I'm just thinking 'A pox on both their houses'."

Smith shook his head, laughing, "You gotta pick one or the other, unless you're just gonna sit on your ass and not vote."

"I know," Will said, "But sometimes, where the choices are so bad, I just wish that we'd secede and take our toys and go home."

"That's seriously messed up, man," Smith said. "Not me, man. I like being part of the biggest, baddest country in the world."

Will shook his head, "Dude, that would be China. They're the biggest."

Smith took one of his hands off the wheel and gave Will the one finger salute, saying, "You know what I mean. Nobody messes with America, man, nobody."

"I know, Edgar. All I'm saying is that things are seriously messed up. I'm not sure that I have any faith in the system anymore. It's broken and we both know it. But, you know I'm picking up what you're putting down, man. I know for some people things are pretty good, but tell me, do you think it's as good now as it was twenty years ago?"

Smith shrugged his shoulders, "No, I guess not, but it's a far cry better than it was sixty or eighty years ago, at least for a *Pochingo* like me."

Will reflected on that before replying, "Yeah, things were pretty messed up. Sometimes the good old days for some people were the bad old days for others. Still, though, what it would be to see Texas decide to stay independent, and never join the US. We wouldn't have any of this crap in Washington to deal with."

Smith burst out laughing, and finally said, "We'd have kicked your gringo asses out of Texas, that's what would have happened. Mexico *uber alles*!"

Will scowled at his driver before saying, "Last time I checked, your ass is half-gringo, too."

Smith glanced over at Will and coyly replied, "Smartass. What do you want me to say? Remember the Alamo? I don't think so."

Will responded to his driver with his own one finger salute.

As the convoy continued down the sand covered road, the sandstorm returned with a vengeance. After flipping the switch and turning the windshield wipers on, Smith said, "God, I wish this deployment was over. You got a job waiting for you when you return?"

Will wistfully replied, "Not yet, man. I thought I had it all figured out. After 9/11 I dropped out of Galveston College and joined up. Did my four years active then decided to finish my next four by joining you nasty girls, while I finished my degree at U of H. I had completed my student teaching and thought I had lined up a gig teaching Texas history in Baytown, when Uncle Sam decided to Charlie Foxtrot all over my plans. Now I get to start the application process all over. What about you?"

"I think so; my Dad said that the housing market's really slowing down. He's worried that home construction's drying up, but if he's still contracting when I get home, I'll go back to work for him."

The sandstorm increased in intensity and they returned to watching the road, as the convoy ate away the miles to the forward operating base. The brake lights on the truck in front of them came on and they slowed down. Will stared out the passenger window at the road's edge, where the sand stirred and billowed, making it difficult to see. As the truck in front of them slammed on the brakes, Will strained to see out the window, as Smitty reacted by bringing the Humvee to a sudden stop. The sand eddying around dropped visibility to just a few feet. Toward the front of the convoy he heard a loud pop followed a moment later by the staccato sound of a heavy machine gun going off.

Smith swore and gripped the steering wheel. He jerked the wheel hard to the right, attempting to steer around the truck. As the right front wheel edged off the road, Will's world turned upside down. An improvised explosive device detonated as the wheel rolled over the triggering mechanism. Will came to a moment later, hanging upside down in his harness. His rifle hung down toward the roof, dangling from its sling. He could feel the ground shaking with explosions but all he could hear was a steady ringing in his ears. He twisted around in his harness and saw Sergeant Smith suspended in his harness. The grunt's patrol cap lay on the Humvee's ceiling. It appeared to Will that his companion's head had slammed against the driver's side window, as blood dripped onto the roof of the vehicle.

Will fumbled with the latch on his harness as he tried to release it, but his hands would not respond to the commands his brain sent. He thought it strange, but as his hand fell away from the clasp on the harness, his thoughts became jumbled. As he tried to keep his eyes focused on Smitty, in some part of his brain he knew something was horribly wrong, as the image of his friend, suspended upside down in his harness, retreated into the distance, pulling away until only the black was left.

Dust filled the air as soldiers secured the area around the convoy. Several vehicles were on fire, black smoke billowing into the blue sky. A couple of men from the stalled truck in front of the overturned Humvee ran back, looking through the cracked windshield and saw Staff Sergeant Travers and Sergeant Smith hanging upside down from their harnesses. A small puddle of blood pooled on the vehicle's roof, under Smith. They tried opening the passenger door but the frame was bent, and no matter how much effort they put into prying it open, it refused to budge. They ducked when a loud staccato sound from a machine gun roared over the sound of crackling flames.

Worried about the men trapped inside the overturned Humvee, one of the soldiers ran around to the driver's side door and tried the handle. The door swung out, letting the man see Sergeant Smith hanging by his harness, blood dripping from a deep gash in his scalp. In the distance, ahead of the convoy a crescendo of gunfire caused the soldier to crawl into the cab, holding Smith up while he unfastened the harness. As the unresponsive driver fell into the soldier's arms, he dragged him from the vehicle and lay him on the side of the road.

He breathed a sigh of relief when the sound of the gunfight ahead of the convey seemed to move away from the vehicles. Breathing a little easier, he crawled back into the cab and released Staff Sergeant Travers from his harness. He pulled him from the Humvee and dragged him next to Smith. A medic, with a drab green patch with an embroidered black cross fixed to his left sleeve, knelt beside Travers. Aside from a few scrapes, the medic couldn't readily find anything wrong. He felt for a pulse and found it. He leaned in and saw the unconscious man was breathing normally. He moved over to Sergeant Smith, whose scalp was lacerated, where it had slammed against the window.

As the sound of the firefight dissipated, the medic, with help from nearby soldiers, transferred the injured into the back of a M923 cargo truck. The disabled vehicles were pushed to the side of the road and the convoy continued to the Forward Operating Base. In addition to Travers and Smith, another member of their company was wounded, and the three were transported by medivac to the Air Force Theater

Hospital Balad, north of Baghdad. It was the largest US military hospital in the country.

Staff Sergeant Travers' minor injuries were quickly bandaged, but he remained unresponsive. The medical staff performed an MRI and found swelling on the brain, which explained why Travers remained in a coma. Stabilized, Travers and his fellow Texas Army National Guardsmen were transferred to Germany where they were treated at Landstuhl Regional Medical Center. Sergeant Edgar Smith's injury quickly healed and physically he soon rebounded and was transferred stateside within a couple of weeks of the attack on the convoy. Before the end of the year, he was medically discharged due to chronic migraines as a result from the head injury.

The doctors at Landstuhl couldn't bring Staff Sergeant Travers out of his coma, even after the swelling on the brain went down. As the largest US military hospital in Europe, there was no shortage of experts who cycled through Travers' room, reviewed the extensive testing and ordered more. There were plenty of doctors who explained in detail what they expected to happen. Those, either humbler or who better understood their own limits, shrugged and admitted they didn't know why Travers lingered in his coma.

After a few months, he was transferred to Brooke Army Medical Center in Texas, where new doctors ordered more tests and waited for the young staff sergeant to awaken. Ellis and Sharon Travers, the young soldier's parents made the three-hour drive between Galveston and San Antonio often, hoping and praying that he would one day wake up.

He heard someone moving around and indiscernible voices babbling in the distance. Like a rubber band snapping, he was pulled toward the sounds around him. He jerked his eyes open, expecting to see the bright lights of a hospital room and doctors and nurses rushing about. Instead he shivered as he felt a frigid wind blow across his face. He saw the sky overhead, orange and red hues bursting from behind a smattering of clouds, as he watched it lighten. The first coherent thoughts to run through his brain were "Where's Smitty? Where are the doctors? Am I outside a field hospital?"

Cold seeped into his body, and he irreverently thought "Heaven's a hell of a lot colder than I expected." Then he saw the sun cresting above a nearby grove of live oak trees. Next, he noticed his breath in the wintery air. Shivering, he found he was lying on the cold, hard ground, wrapped in an itchy, navy blue woolen blanket. The pain he had anticipated as he made his first, tenuous movements was absent. He pulled back the blanket, which smelled faintly of smoke, and stood and noticed that he was wearing a light blue pair of woolen pants and thick gray wool socks. His shirt was white muslin fabric, not unlike the backing on the curtains he remembered hanging in the window of his parents' home. A fire burned nearby, where several men were trying to warm up. Each of them, it seemed to Will, dressed similarly to himself. The ringing in his ears was gone and he heard horses close by. He turned around until he saw a string of several dozen horses along a rope picket, their breathing filling the air around them with frosty vapor.

Will's mind rebelled against the staggering images

before his eyes. *"Where the hell am I?"* Will's mind screamed. He fell to the blanket, as his head thundered with pain, feeling like his brain was being ripped open. Blood pounded in his ears and his temples throbbed, as he barely managed to hold on to consciousness. Like a vast waterfall, suddenly memories not his own cascaded into his mind, flooding it with recollections clashing with those of his own. Like a man drowning in water far over his head, he grasped at the first thought to coalesce in his mind, as though grabbing a life preserver. He saw a young, dark haired, beautiful woman. A name came unbidden, Rosanna, his wife. *"Stop!"* His mind cried out, *"I'm not married!"* He seized firmly at what he knew to be true. No, he wasn't married, didn't even have a girlfriend currently. Another memory floated to the surface of his mind. A painful divorce from Rosanna. But the thought wasn't completely full of pain. He remembered a son, Charlie, a vision of a red haired little boy, no more than three or four, came to mind. He said, "What the hell? I don't have a son?" Will clamped his mouth with his hands when he realized he spoke aloud, shutting it as he tried desperately to reconcile the flood of bizarre memories with what he knew to be his own life. Was it fact competing with fiction or was something larger happening to him?

He lay back on the woolen blanket from his sitting position, both hands clutching his head, his mind continued to rebel in pain as the divergent memories competed for space in his overwhelmed mind. One of the men standing nearby, noticed and came over to him, calling out, "Colonel, are you alright?"

"Colonel? Oh, hell no! I'm no colonel. Officers suck and I want no part of that, thank you very much!" But

thankfully, the only words that escaped his lips were, "Yeah, Private Smithers. I'll be fine, just a bit of a headache." With an audible sigh, Will thought, "Okay. I've never heard that voice in my life, but my mouth seems to be working, but those were certainly not my thoughts. Can this really be happening to me?"

What 'this' was he didn't have a clue, but he took a deep breath to settle his nerves and paused a moment to search through the new memories swirling around inside his head. Something his brain identified as a recent memory showed a two-room house. The rooms were divided by a dogtrot. *"How the hell do I know what a dogtrot is?"* He thought. The first room held a fireplace with cooking utensils hung nearby, and a table and a bed. The utensils appeared to be seldom used, as dust coated each piece of pewter. Across the dirt packed dogtrot, the second room held a few law books on a crude bookshelf affixed to the wall and another rough-hewn table in the middle of the room. *"That's something,"* Will thought, *"But who the hell's thoughts are running rampant through my head?"*

As though responding to a query, his mind brought into focus another memory. Will saw himself, not as the five foot eleven, twenty-seven-year-old part-time National Guard soldier from Galveston, with dirty blond hair, and aspirations of teaching Texas history. Instead, the image was that of a six foot one red-haired, blue-eyed man, standing across a rough table from another man dressed in a long, brown topcoat, a colorfully checkered vest, and a white starched shirt, with brown woolen pants. It reminded him of a painting he saw when he was a child, touring the state capital on a school field trip. The other man spoke, "Colonel Travis, I reject out of hand your request that I relieve you of command. We both thought that you'd find more men to fill out a regiment of cavalry, but we were wrong. So many men are already assembled, that there just aren't that many waiting around to enlist, and God alone knows when more volunteers from back east will arrive. Nevertheless, you will take your men to join up with Colonel Neill, and if expedient, help him transfer the cannon from Bexar back here to Washington-on-the-Brazos. Consult with Neill and if it's possible, destroy the Mission San Antonio de Valero while you're at it."

As the memory played in his head, Will felt the soldier's sense of shame as he replied, "Yes, sir. Governor Smith. It's just that I've only managed to collect twenty-nine men. I thought for certain I would collect a couple of hundred to join the regular cavalry." The older man waved the complement away, and the soldier continued, "I hope that between these and Colonel Neill's we'll have enough to get the job done."

As that memory coalesced with the myriad of others swirling around in Will's very crowded head, an icy wind twirled across his skin, and chills ran down his spine. The words he had spoken to Sergeant Smith replayed in his mind, *"what I wouldn't give to see Texas decide to go its own way and never join the US."* Was he in a coma and dreaming a vivid dream? Was the universe playing tricks on him, and this simply a cosmic joke? Or had God, in an act of perfect schadenfreude, decided to strand him in the worst of possible times? Even if this body wasn't his own, he knew to whom it belonged, and understood all too well what it meant to inhabit the body of William Barret Travis. He grasped at Travis' most recent memories and knew it was the 1st of February 1836. With a cascading sense of finality, everything in his mind fell into place at that point. In

2008 the Mission San Antonio de Valero had another name that is known throughout the world. The Alamo.

Will closed his eyes, resisting the temptation to curl into a fetal position on the blanket, wondering at whether it was fate or God that would throw his mind back in history. He hoped with every fiber in his body all this was nothing more than a dream. *"Yes,"* he thought, *"That's it. My body is in a coma from the explosion."* And if that were so, he would eventually wake up. He pinched himself, and nothing happened. He pinched a lot harder. "Damn!" he muttered, "That hurt." Nothing changed. He was still sitting on an itchy, woolen blanket on a freezing February morning in 1836. Even though his mind accepted he was dreaming, he couldn't help but work out the details of what would happen if this were real. He quickly calculated, February 1 to March 6. Thirty-four days. No, it's a leap year. Thirty-five days until the Alamo falls. He stood again, shakily, as his legs seemed determined to drop him back down. He couldn't decide if this was all a dream but until he woke up, he would go through the motions as if this was real. He was uncertain about so many things he knew he would need to figure out. But on one issue he was determined. Forget the Alamo! He wouldn't be waiting there on March 6, 1836.

Chapter 2

Will pulled on a blue, waist length jacket. He fingered the gold cloth stars sewn on each collar, giving the jacket a distinct military flair. Chilled, he flapped his arms, trying to get his blood flowing in the frigid air. He saw a half-dozen men crowded around the warmth of a campfire. From there, he looked around the large campsite and saw the rest of the men, either packing gear or huddled around one of several fires. With more than a little awe at the innumerable memories competing for space in his pounding, hurting head, he plucked one from the previous day and 'recalled', if 'recall' was the correct word, that he and the thirty others were only forty miles from San Antonio.

Will sensed William B. Travis expected to arrive at the Alamo on the 3rd of February, two days hence. With no idea how he was 'recalling' these memories from Travis, Will did the only thing that made sense, he set aside wondering how it was happening and hoped that the pounding in his head would subside if he just didn't let the paradox get to him, if all this wasn't just a dream. The thought that Travis intended to take two more days to arrive at the Alamo bemused Will, as he considered the training he had received as an infantryman. He could march forty miles in two days without a problem, he thought. With horses, it seemed likely that he could get there no later than midafternoon on the 2nd of February, rather than the 3rd. *"Still, though,"* Will thought, *"If this is no dream, I'd be a fool not to consider these men that are trusting Travis to get them there safely. It's no empty refrain to say it's not what we don't know that gets us into trouble, but what we know that ain't so."* Unsure if there was any comfort to be found in that thought, Will walked toward the nearest campfire.

As he approached, one of the men, the only black man among the entire company, as best as Will could tell, approached him, and said, "Marse William, sir, here's your coffee." The ebony skinned man's name came unbidden into Will's mind as he accepted the steaming brew. "Thanks, Joe." Joe's eyes arched up in surprise at Will's comment. *"Damn. First few words I've spoken, and already I've put my foot in it."* As he watched Joe return to the campfire, Will played the interaction in his mind repeatedly, until it dawned on him his mistake was the gentle word of thanks he had spoken to Joe. Will discovered no memory of Travis being a cruel master, but neither did Travis ask or thank Joe for any services provided. It simply never crossed his mind to ask, thank, or praise a slave.

Will watched Joe assist in the cooking around the campfire. He felt his stomach sharply contract as he wrestled with the invading memories of William B. Travis, as they contested with Will's own values and beliefs. If, as he feared, God inflicted a cosmic curse on him, and he was truly stranded in the body of this long dead martyr of the Texas Revolution, he couldn't wrap his mind around *owning* another human being. As a product of the twenty-first century, he was too far removed from the antebellum worldview of men like Travis and other Southerners of the mid-nineteenth century. As a student of history, the words from an even earlier era seeped into his consciousness. It was self-evident that all men were created equal and endowed by their creator with certain inalienable rights, such as life, liberty and the pursuit of happiness. He bit his lip, remembering that those words were penned by Thomas Jefferson, who was himself a slave owner. For a moment, it was like being back in the Humvee with Smitty, recalling that, for too many, the good old days were worse than for others. Allowing that to sink in, it was startling clear that the 6th of March was just around the corner and if he was at the Alamo on that day, the good old days would be far worse for one Will Travers.

As a Texas history buff, Will considered himself knowledgeable about the Revolutionary period in Texas and he knew that there were still more than three weeks until the siege of the Alamo began, so even if he stayed the course and continued to the Alamo, as William B. Travis had intended, there was still plenty of time to gather up the cannon and get back to east Texas, like Travis and Governor Smith had discussed a few weeks prior. He nodded his head imperceptibly, and felt a little better about things, until his eyes fell back on the slave, Joe. He closed his eyes briefly, thinking, "Please God, let this be a dream."

Never in his life had Will felt as conflicted as he did at that moment. Even though he couldn't acknowledge this was really happening to him, and thought this all still likely to be a dream, he could never have imagined that if this were really happening to him he would be cast into the winds of history, transforming his mind into the body of a nineteenth century lawyer, soldier, and worse yet, as far as Will was concerned, martyr. Nor could he reconcile himself to the nearly alien worldview whirling around in his head, thanks to the fusing going on between the memories of William B. Travis and his own.

Even since his days at Galveston College, nearly a decade previous, when he took History 101, he considered himself a historian, if for no other reason, than his passion for the subject. In many of his previous conversations with professors, other students, or his buddies in the National Guard, he had argued that judging people in the past solely on twenty-first century values held by reasonably enlightened people was wrong. Rather, he had argued, they should be judged based upon their actions when compared to the prevailing beliefs of their own time. This was the primary reason Will could look at Thomas Jefferson and feel only a slight chagrin that he could pen such an incredible and inspiring defense of liberty as was found in the Declaration of Independence while simultaneously owning another human soul. Yet, there Will Travers stood on that windswept Texas prairie in the body of William B. Travis, chilled to the bone, and found he had no option but to acknowledge that he could not, in his heart, bow to that one peculiar view held by William B. Travis, as well as by countless others that one could own as a chattel another human being.

Mentally, he pushed against the memories of Travis and he clawed toward his own, and found the one for which he searched. He was a young teenager, sitting in a Sunday school classroom. A quote had been written across a chalkboard. "You may choose to look the other way but you can never say again that you did not know." The quote, he recalled, was from William Wilberforce. The class had read a modern adaptation of Wilberforce's book Real Christianity, which had resonated in his adolescent heart. During college, his interest in church waned; although Wilberforce's passionate faith had always struck a chord in Will's heart. If memory served him correctly, Wilberforce fought against the slave trade twenty or thirty years earlier than the time Will considered the 'here and now'. This was the frame of reference Will was looking for. Relief settled on Will, like a blanket covering a newborn, and he knew if this were not just a dream but his new reality, he would oppose the evil he knew slavery to be, not by applying any twenty-first century anachronistic view, but by embracing the views of men like William Wilberforce. There was something else that dawned on him, as he reveled in this comforting thought. He knew something that millions of other Southerners didn't in 1836. Slavery was on its way out. Will didn't know how or when but he vowed to do whatever was within his power to hasten its demise.

There was only one minuscule problem to overcome, Will realized as he went to check on Travis' horse. Somehow or another he had to survive the Alamo.

Will had thought riding in a dusty Humvee was one of the less pleasant ways of traveling, but after spending more than fifteen hours over the last day and a half watching from his saddle the ears of his horse twitch, he changed his mind. He tried adjusting his position in the saddle, but no matter how he sat, his backside was intensely sore. He wondered how much worse he would feel about it, if the body he inhabited was not accustomed to the intense rigors of nineteenth century frontier life. "*Chalk up one positive thing*." Will thought as he added to this list in his head the good and bad of his present predicament.

Nearly two days in the saddle gave Will time to put to rest the idea he was just dreaming. While he couldn't disprove it, the fact he had yet to awaken from this surreal situation, argued he should behave as though what he experienced was real. As he accepted this new reality, the realization he would never see his parents, friends or fellow National Guardsmen again hit hard. As he swayed in the saddle, guiding the horse along the wagon road, the hardest thing to accept was he would never see his parents again.

The highlight of each week in Iraq had been the short Skype calls where he would catch up with his parents, telling them about the funny things that would happen in camp while glossing over the inherent risks. There would be no more Skype calls. No hope that when this war was over he would return to them. There was something heartbreakingly final as he accepted the loss, as he rode along in silence, mourning it.

The time on the trail also allowed him time to start compartmentalizing William B. Travis' memories from his own and to think about his future. His first inclination was to tell Joe he was a free man then tell the men with whom he was riding that to continue to the Alamo was a death sentence. If they were smart, like him, they would turn their horses around and ride like hell to the east. His lips twitched up in a ghost of a smile as he allowed that first impulse to replay across his mind. Somewhere along the way, it crossed his mind that in a way, this was like a disagreement that he had with a professor when he was finishing up his degree. He recalled receiving a grade he thought was unfair and in a fit of pique he pounded out exactly what he had thought about the grade and his professor, in no uncertain terms. When he read the email back to himself there was immense satisfaction. When he placed the cursor over the send button, he relished the catharsis of getting his ire out of his system. But rather than sending his screed to the professor, he moved the cursor to the delete button and clicked on it. He had learned some thoughts were at their best when they remained locked in his mind.

He ruminated that the time on the trail was akin to that cathartic email exercise. At first, he railed against God, for nature would never be so cruel. If this were no dream, then his entire world had been upended. His mind had been cast adrift in a sea of time, washing ashore at a point in history far more dangerous than the time from which he came.

That thought had barely coalesced before a couple of men riding near him turned, looking inquisitively at their commander. "Colonel, you all right?" one rider asked.

Will realized these men heard him laugh. How could he think that this was more dangerous, when he had nearly been killed by an IED in Iraq? He waved to the riders, saying, "It was nothing, Smithers. Just thinking."

Danger was relative, he realized. Being stranded in Travis' body may not be the healthiest of situations, but apart from waking up from this nightmare, it was where he now found himself. Dreaming of turning tail and telling fate to go take a hike was his 'send button.'

"Come on, snowflake," Will thought, *"you know that any comfort zone is nothing but an illusion. If God, in his infinite mysteriousness, saw fit to do this to me, I doubt that turning tail and running for the hills is what I should do. If it was nothing more than fate and randomness that did this, then fate is a fickle mistress, and the best revenge is living the life of William B. Travis as well and as long as possible."*

He decided running away was the wrong course of action. This left Will in a quandary. *"What do I do next?"* An amusing thought came to mind, and he bit his tongue to keep from laughing out loud. He could have been stranded at any point in history. He could have found himself in Louis the XVI's body. He knew little French history and spoke the language not at all. Or worse, trapped in the body of Joseph Stalin. As unsavory as some of William B. Travis' memories were, there was no trace of insanity in them. As a matter of fact, Will mused, as a self-professed Texas history nut, he knew more than most about the battles of the Texas Revolution. One thing he knew for certain was that trying to defend the old mission was about as close as you could come in the nineteenth century to suicide by cop. He took stock of what else he knew and recalled that on the 2nd of February Colonel Neill was holding the Alamo and San Antonio with less than a hundred men. Jim Bowie should have already arrived with another fifty and Crockett perhaps a week from now with another dozen or so. Will calculated that would give the Texian force only about 150 men, give or take a few. Against that, Santa Anna would arrive with nearly two thousand soldiers far earlier than anyone anticipated, on the 23rd of February. *"Only now,"* thought Will, *"I know it, so it is anticipated."*

There was another piece of the puzzle which tickled the back of Will's mind. He couldn't remember if it was from the old John Wayne *Alamo* movie or the newer one with Billy Bob Thornton, but it was mentioned that the old mission had the most artillery in one location west of the Mississippi. Will wasn't sure how many guns were mounted on the walls, but it must have been upward of twenty. Those guns could prove useful. He wondered if there were any men at the Alamo with the necessary skills to use them effectively.

His thoughts were interrupted as Will's small troop of mounted soldiers crested a low rise. Several miles in the distance, he could see the walls of the old mission standing defiantly against a terrain that seemed unable to make up its mind whether it was prairie or desert. As they continued along the road, he could see that the walls of the Alamo were low; they appeared to be no more than eight or ten feet in height. He shook his head slightly as he examined the walls in greater detail. *"Heaven help us,"* he thought, *"even a midget pole-vaulter could clear those walls."*

Wearing his best expression, Will turned around, facing the men who were following him and said, "It was started as a mission, but it doesn't look much like a church. Those walls, they don't much make it look like a fort, either. But damned if sitting out there on the prairie, it isn't just a little bit impressive!"

The men smiled and laughed in agreement. They had been confused by their leader's uncharacteristic silence over the past couple of days, and they were encouraged to hear something that sounded like the old Travis who had led them over the past few weeks.

Approaching the old mission, Will observed the Alamo's gate had been reinforced with a lunette, with two artillery pieces entrenched, in a manner similar to what he recalled in the most recent Alamo movie. Eyeballing the lunette, it appeared to Will it was intended to provide fire support to the low walls to both sides of the gatehouse. But further to the right of the gate, where he recalled there being a short wooden palisade, the ground was open. There was no wall between the sally port and the iconic mission. It was then that he recalled the wooden palisade was erected after Travis had arrived. Will and his men threaded their way through the lunette and passed through the sally port into the Alamo's large plaza.

Will slowly dismounted from the horse with relief. The hours spent in the saddle had not been kind to his backside. There were no men standing on parade, nor was there any band to welcome their arrival. Several men looked up from their work as he and his men filed into the plaza. A few waved at Will and his men before returning to their work, where they were reinforcing a section of the wall with heavy wooden posts. From a two-story building Will recalled as the hospital, a tall, heavyset man wearing a long, blue frock coat came down the stairs, followed by a heavy scent of pipe tobacco clinging to his clothes. His wavy, light brown hair and thick sideburns stood in stark contrast to his ruddy complexion.

From the memories of Travis, Will recognized the Alamo's commanding officer, Colonel James Neill. He wore a wide smile as he extended his hand and shook Will's. "Buck!" Neill said, "It is damned good to see you, man!" Despite himself, Will couldn't resist the older man's enthusiasm. He couldn't decide if it was because of Travis' formality or Will's own experience in the army, but he drew himself up to his full height and gave the garrison's commander a sharp salute. A smile creased his face and he replied, "Colonel, it is truly good to be seen by eyes as sore as your own." Neill beckoned Will to follow him as he started back toward the stairs. His foot was on the first step when he turned and said, "Tell me that this is only your vanguard. Surely the remainder of your command is on the way."

Chapter 3

Will stopped in his tracks, and sputtered, "Vanguard?" He knew William B. Travis had spent the time since the Texian army had captured San Antonio at the end of the previous year trying to recruit a cavalry battalion. Despite Travis' best effort, all he had to show for it were the twenty-nine men who were dismounting from their horses behind Will. Colonel Neill noticed Will's crestfallen face and heaved a heavy sigh. "Damn Johnson and Grant to hell! Had those fools not cleared out our garrison on that stupid Matamoros scheme, we'd be in a sight better position, Colonel Travis."

Will recalled few details from his Texas history about the Matamoros expedition, other than it was a failure which ultimately diluted the strength of the Revolutionary army around San Antonio. He glanced around the plaza and saw Neill's men were entrenching more than a dozen cannon along and atop the walls ringing the plaza. He wondered what the expedition had cost the garrison, so he asked, "What all did Johnson and Grant take when they left?"

Colonel Neill started back up the stairs, and said,

"My office is up here, why don't you join me? I'll get you current with things."

As Neill took a seat across a rough-hewn desk, he gestured Will to a high-backed wooden chair on the opposite side of the desk. He replied, "I don't really mind the four cannons that they set off with. As you can see, we've got plenty of artillery in the Alamo. But they took most of the supplies that we captured from Cos, when we sent him skedaddling back into Mexico."

As Colonel Neill talked, it dawned on Will that there were certain gaps between what he knew of the Texas Revolution and William B. Travis' memories. None of the information in his memories told him how many men had followed Johnson and Grant, nor how serious a dent they had put in the Alamo's supplies. Knowing the lore of the Texas Revolution wasn't enough, he realized. He couldn't help wondering if the holes in his knowledge would trip him up as he tried to maneuver through the revolution and survive. He realized then Neill was still talking when he heard, "and what do you think of that, Buck?"

"Ah, well, there were not many able-bodied men left to recruit, Colonel Neill. Most of them are either with us here, or with Fannin or further south with Grant and Johnson." Will paused for a moment and noticed Neill leaning in waiting for him to continue, "Of course Houston is back east of the Brazos recruiting as many men as he can, but in my opinion, he's more concerned with making sure the provisional government declares independence than raising an army."

Colonel Neill nodded his head and replied, "That, I fear, is the sad, sorry truth, Buck, but ever since Stephen Austin returned from his imprisonment in Mexico City, my belief is that Centralism will triumph in

Mexico and the ideals of federalism are dead. Houston's right, I think. Independence is our only course of action now."

That suited Will just fine. After passing on a cigar Neill offered, he watched as the other officer took a pipe from a pocket, filled it with aromatic tobacco and lit it. He decided now was as good a time as any to ask his own million-dollar question. "Where do things stand regarding General Houston's command to dismantle the Alamo and bring the artillery east?"

He watched Neill's expression carefully, as the other man puffed on the pipe and blew a smoke ring into the air. After an extended pause Colonel Neill responded, "Now, Buck, I was under the impression Sam had given us discretion about fortifying the Alamo here or taking the guns with us back east."

Will cocked an eyebrow at Neill, and with his voice heavy with skepticism asked, "Do you really think we can hold this old mission, James?'

"I was pretty much set to start pulling down the walls here when Jim Bowie arrived a couple of weeks ago. He and I have talked about it and believe we can make the Alamo defensible. We have twenty-two guns with enough powder and loads to make a fine showing of things. But I doubt it will come to that. I'm certain Sam will arrive here with the army before Santa Anna arrives," Neill said.

Will was searching for the right words with which to respond when a shadow fell across the door as another man entered the room. Equal in height to both Colonel Neill and Will, with wavy light-brown hair that was starting to recede, Jim Bowie filled the doorway. Will felt more than a little awe at the man. Jim Bowie radiated a feral fierceness and charisma. Will glanced down at the huge blade hanging at Bowie's belt and instinctively he knew the stories about Bowie's formidable skills with the blade were more than mere legends. Bowie nodded to Will and smiled, "Buck, how was San Filipe?"

Forgetting what he was about to say to Neill, Will was momentarily taken aback by Bowie's friendly gesture. He mentally rifled through Travis' memories until he recalled Jim Bowie had used Travis' legal services on several land deals over the past few years. More than that, the two were on friendly terms. Once again it hit home, in Will's mind, that what one learns in the history books isn't always the whole truth. Will smiled back, happy some things appeared to be different than expected, and said with a wave in Bowie's direction, "Evenin' Jim. Truth be told, there are hardly any men of military age in the settlement. Most are with Houston, Fannin, or with those fools Grant and Johnston down south of here."

Bowie acknowledged Will's wave with a nod of his head and sat on the edge of the table, between Will and Colonel Neill. He said, "One of my boys returned from Grant's camp. Right now, he's down around Refugio. It looks like Grant's finding it rough going. Most of the men who rode south with him are with Fannin now. But where that jumped-up dandy is right now is anybody's guess."

Will smiled, when he realized he knew something the other two men didn't. "Jim, I heard tell that Fannin's at Goliad."

Bowie quirked an eyebrow up, and said, "Do tell."

Will froze up for a moment, when he realized neither Travis' memories nor his own knowledge of history was much help to him. He shrugged his shoulders and made an educated guess, saying, "Not much to tell, just heard back in San Filipe that he stopped there. Maybe he's waiting for Grant to tell him they're welcome in Matamoros." For a moment Will wondered if it was a poor idea to offer up speculation and recalled, it's not what you don't know that will get you into trouble, it's what you know that isn't so that will do you in. Will fervently hoped his guess was good.

With the other officers' attention firmly fixed on Will, he figured if they had accepted one nugget they could be receptive to another. Maybe with the roll of the dice he could do something about their futures. He pointed to a large map spread across the desk and asked, "What are the odds Santa Anna is marching north with his army sooner than we expect?"

While Jim Bowie scratched his chin, thinking about the question, Colonel Neill barely refrained from sneering when he replied, "The Mexican army? Marching in this weather? I can't imagine him getting here before the spring. He's at least six to eight weeks away. Why would Santa Anna risk the attrition of marching his army north in the dead of winter? When he arrives, Houston will be here with his army."

Will wasn't surprised by Neill's response. He knew most armies didn't fancy marching in the winter time, and 1836 had proven to be a colder one than most, he recalled. He cocked his head to Bowie, and asked, "What do you think, Jim?"

From his perch on the edge of the table, Bowie gave a thoughtful look and said, "Normally I'd agree with James," Bowie nodded to Neill, acknowledging his given name. "But with Tamaulipas in near revolt, Santa Anna may decide to bleed his army in his haste to come north. If he does that, why, he could be here inside two weeks."

Colonel Neill replied, "Jim, do you really think Santa Anna can mobilize the Mexican army and march them across the northern desert in the dead of winter? That seems a bit much, don't you think?"

Bowie shot up from the desk, and fired back at Neill, "Why? Because they're Mexicans? Don't tell me you think they're all a bit on the lazy side, James. These are my wife's people you're talking about. They may be laid-back and relaxed, but when they get their dander up, they get things done. And one thing about Santa Anna, you can bet his dander is most certainly up."

Neill worked up a smile in response to Bowie's volcanic outburst, "Jim, that isn't what I meant. I just don't think it's conceivable he could march his army north through the dead of winter."

Before Bowie could say anything more, Will chose that moment to interject, "Respectfully, James," he said to Neill, "I'm glad our own General Knox didn't feel the same way about the abilities of the Continental soldiers he commanded when he brought those big guns from Ticonderoga to Boston back in 1775 in the dead of winter." Will said a silent prayer of thanks he was a history buff, and had that little gem rattling in his head.

Neill grew silent and swiveled his eyes between Will and Bowie, then gave a self-deprecating laugh. "I take both of your points, gentlemen. I don't want to give the Mexican army the same due that I'd give our own Continentals. If General Howe hadn't done the same, we might all still be British subjects. Damned if I'm going to fall into the same trap." He sighed heavily as he conceded the point before asking, "So, Buck, what are you proposing?"

Since shortly after waking up in Travis' body, Will

had been thinking about the next step. He knew he needed to carefully lay out the strategy which would get all of them out from behind Alamo's walls. He cautiously laid out his plan, saying "First, it is imperative we find out when Santa Anna brings his army across the Rio Grande River. Also, where he intends to cross. Personally, I think the most likely route is along the Camino Real. Wouldn't it be something if we could entrench our artillery along the ford where the Camino crosses the Rio Grande? I bet we could stop Santa Anna dead in his tracks."

Bowie slapped Will on the back, saying, "Damnation, Buck, I like the way you think. It had never crossed my mind the Rio Grande would be the best place to stop Santa Anna. Hell, men, if we could put a hundred riflemen on the Rio Grande along with some of these cannons, we'd have three or four hundred yards of clear fire. I bet ol' Santa Anna will lead out with those lancers of his. If we can remove those pieces from the chess board, a determined force could cause Santa Anna to stall out there and bleed for several days."

Will shot up in his cot, his eyes flying open as he abruptly awoke. He had hoped being in the saddle for so much of the last couple of days would help him sleep. But his rest had been troubled with dreams. The one which startled him awake, was just the latest in a long procession of dreams troubling his sleep. Not wanting to close his eyes, he swung his feet onto the floor and stood, wrapping the woolen blanket around him as he stepped over to the small window facing the Alamo Plaza and cracked the shutter open, looking into the inky darkness. He guessed the sun would peek over the eastern horizon shortly. He was ready for the day. The dreams were an assortment of his and Travis'. The one which had awakened him had found himself back in the wreck of the Humvee. The engine was on fire and ammunition was cooking off in the rear seat. When he turned to Sergeant Smitty all he saw was a skeleton staring back at him. When he looked out the shattered windows, there were dozens of men milling around, ignoring the burning vehicle. They were all dressed like the men in the Alamo. No matter how loud he cried out not a single head turned in his direction. He felt the heat from the fire getting hotter and winced each time a round of ammunition cooked off behind him. He turned back and tried to shake the skeleton, but as he reached out his hands, the mass of bones turned to face him and he heard the distinct voice of the sergeant say, "Save me!"

He screamed and tried unfastening the harness holding him in place. As the clasp gave way and he fell onto the roof of the Humvee, he looked back toward the milling men. As one, they turned their ghoulish faces, frozen in an anguished and tortured death. In unison they chimed, "Save us!"

Will awoke at that point. He wasn't one to see messages in dreams but he couldn't shake the images seared into his mind. He shivered, pulling the blanket, draped around his shoulders, closer in around his neck. It felt like another cold day was about to dawn. For a moment he wondered how he would adjust to a summer in Texas without air conditioning. He shrugged his shoulders and decided he needed to worry about surviving the coming weeks. Summer was still a long way off.

After exiting the tiny room assigned to him, Will ran

into Joe, who was holding a steaming mug of coffee. The slave bobbed his head and handed him the coffee, saying, "Here you go, Marse William."

Will accepted the coffee and thanked Joe. On one hand, part of him was amused at Joe's attempt to cover his surprise at Will's thanks. But conversely, it angered him that Joe was trapped in a life of slavery and William B. Travis was complicit. Feeling his anger starting to rise, Will tamped it down, saying to himself, *"One thing at a time 'Buck.' Gotta win first before tackling other important stuff."* He compartmentalized this and walked across the plaza looking for whoever commanded the artillery.

A little while later Will was finding out many things are easier said than done. Refining yesterday's plan into something which would work was tough going. He had found the Alamo's artillery was under the command of a couple of different officers, which made little sense to him. That was how he found himself talking to Captains Almaron Dickinson and William Carey. Carey leaned against a small field cannon, saying, "There are twelve artillery pieces we could haul down to the Rio Grande. We have six 6-pounders, four 4-pounders and two 3-pounders. The rest of our ordnance is too large a caliber to transport."

When Carey finished, Dickinson added, "We're critically short of solid shot and exploding shells, but thanks to several shipments last month we have enough powder to sustain a bit of a barrage. What Captain Carey and I have devised are these canister loads. Mostly just rusty nails, broken bits of horseshoes, and of course, musket balls. But we have enough scrap metal for more than two hundred loads, and that still leaves us adequately supplied with powder for our rifles and muskets."

This sounded better than he had hoped. Then Dickinson continued, "The fly in the ointment will be transportation, Colonel Travis." Will winced at the comment. He knew it was too good to be true. Dickinson continued, "The Alamo garrison only has a few horses, certainly not enough to transport a dozen cannon down the Camino Real."

Will felt, more than saw, a presence behind him and turned to see Jim Bowie standing a few feet away. His deep voice boomed, "Are y'all done with the boring stuff yet, Buck?" A smile on Bowie's face and a glimmer in his eye belied his gruff voice.

Will found it was easy to like being in Bowie's presence. A smile crossed Will's lips as he replied, "Oh, no, Jim, we saved the best for you. Captain Dickinson was just telling me everything with the artillery is fine except for a little fly in the ointment. Not enough horses."

Before Bowie could respond, Captain Carey flashed a malevolent smile and interjected, "My colleague, Almaron, is actually not entirely correct, gentlemen. We actually have the necessary animals to get the cannon down to the Rio Grande."

Will sensed he wasn't going to like what Carey was about to say. The artillery captain continued, "We actually have enough horses." He paused, watching Will and Bowie's expressions. Then he dropped the hammer. "Your men were kind enough to donate them. They just don't know it yet."

The men who Will had led into the Alamo were cavalry and he could well imagine they were not going to like it. Bowie's men were all volunteers with a reputation for poor discipline. He hoped none of them decided to 'un-volunteer' over this. For the briefest of moments Will had an image of Travis and Bowie arguing over whose men would bear the brunt of the requirement. For the first time, he realized it wasn't his twenty-first century combat experience or his training that set him apart from the man whose memories he owned. It was his temperament. While he didn't like what Carey had said, he saw no sense in arguing over it. He didn't say anything and slid a glance over to Bowie. The knife fighter simply scowled and said, "This ain't going to go down easy with my men. Nor yours either, Buck."

Will nodded, and with a sigh said, "I agree, but unless they want to push those cannon all the way to the Rio Grande on foot, I expect they'll agree." Both artillery officers smiled. Carey looked especially happy both Will and Bowie were in agreement about the horses. Will decided it was time to remind Carey that a colonel outranks a captain. He said, "William, you could have all the horses in Texas to haul your cannon, but without a cavalry screen, you could be caught unaware, and that, Captain, would be tragic. Colonel Bowie and I are going to need enough horses left free to mount scouting patrols. The last thing we want is to be caught unaware of Santa Anna's movements."

Carey sagged visibly at the comment, and Will continued, "Let's see if we can keep a company of mounted scouts, maybe forty or so, half, no make it a third regulars and two thirds volunteers. If we can't make everyone happy, at least we can all share equally in the misery."

Carey quickly did the math and grinned when he decided he'd still have enough horses to get the job done. Will looked over at Bowie and noticed a frank look of approval on his face. He thought Bowie had expected Travis would demand that his regular army troops be the scouts. Will could only imagine how Bowie would have howled in protest over such a move. But he neatly defused the situation. He smiled back at Bowie and hoped that unity in command would continue. Will dismissed Carey and Dickinson to make the necessary preparations.

He watched the two artillery officers walk away, in animated conversation, making plans for the pending move. When they turned a corner and disappeared around a building, Will gestured to Bowie and said, "Let's take a walk. That was the easy part." Bowie nodded and fell into step beside him. There had not been much time to think through the next part. As he spoke, he hoped Bowie was a good sounding board. "We need a lot more men with us when we head out to face Santa Anna, Jim." He paused as a thought came to him, "Would you be willing to ask Juan Seguin if he would ride out and recruit as many men as he can between here and the Nueces? Do you think he could raise a company of men given enough time?"

Bowie nodded enthusiastically and replied, "He could arrange to meet us down on the Rio Grande with whatever men he can recruit." Will could see Bowie liked the idea as he continued, "I can ask. If anyone can motivate the Tejanos around here to rise up and join our revolution it's Juan."

In his mind, he imagined a list on a whiteboard, and Will mentally checked the boxes for artillery and more cavalry. The imaginary list grew as he considered how few men defended the Alamo. There really were very few choices about how to grow things. He said, "It is absolutely essential we fold Fannin's men into our own.

I think we'd both feel a lot better about our odds against Santa Anna if we could add those three or four hundred men."

Bowie frowned, shaking his head, "That jumped up popinjay is not going to listen to anything I say, that's a damn sight sure."

Will felt a sense of relief as Travis' memories gave him more details about Fannin than what he recalled from his history books. Better understanding Bowie's dislike for the feckless West Point dropout, Will chose his words with care, "Fannin just needs to be encouraged to listen to reason."

Bowie laughed and slapped his back, then said, "Well, Buck, up until yesterday, I woulda told you to send someone else. You and me usually see about the same, when it comes to reason … we don't. But since you've arrived I've noticed command has changed you, and I gotta say, you're showing yourself to be more …" Bowie paused, looking for the right word, "mature, I suppose."

Will resisted the little part of him who wanted to say, *'What gave me away?'* but instead he smiled and replied. "You might say, this command has truly made me into a new man."

As the two turned back toward the plaza, Bowie asked, "So, when do you leave to fetch Fannin and his men?"

Chapter 4

Will and Bowie's stroll carried them outside the walls of the Alamo, and he stopped on the footbridge spanning the acequia next to the lunette which protected the fort's gate. He looked over at Bowie and chuckled. Bowie turned around and with a sly smile on his face asked, "What?"

"I see what you just did, Jim." Will replied, still laughing. "What makes you think I would have any more luck with Fannin than you or Colonel Neill?"

Still smiling, Bowie replied, "You got any better ideas, Buck? Oh, no doubt Jim Neill could talk Fannin into meeting up with us, but it's going to take everything he and I can do to get our men and cannons down to the Rio Grande. Hell, Buck, just admit it, you're the most expendable, oh, I mean, you're the youngest and can stay in the saddle longer than either me or Neill."

Will looked askance at Bowie, and wryly shaking his head, said, "I suspect you had it right the first time, Jim." He was amused at the ease with which Bowie put him on the spot. As he considered the idea, he was likely the only man other than James Neill who could persuade James Fannin to abandon his quixotic quest to support Grant and Johnson on their ill-fated Matamoros expedition.

He followed behind Bowie as they reentered the Alamo plaza. He entertained a couple of ideas about how to move Fannin to act. He knew he was looking at two very long, hard days in the saddle during which he could work out the details. As he recalled, it was roughly ninety miles from San Antonio to Goliad. The town of Goliad owed its existence to the Presidio La Bahia, an old fort established by the Spanish army in the 1740s.

He and Bowie parted ways as Will headed back to his little room. He sat on the edge of the bed and considered what he thought likely to happen over the next couple of weeks. He knew, if unchecked, Santa Anna would arrive in San Antonio on the 23rd of February, in twenty days. Working backward, Will figured If Santa Anna was pushing his army, he would still need seven days after crossing the Rio Grande to reach San Antonio. That meant Will needed to be on the Rio Grande no later than the 15th. *"If that failed,"* Will said to himself, *"would we have time to fall back to the Nueces River and fortify it?"* The Nueces River was little more than a creek where the Camino Real crossed it. Will counted the cost of failure and silently shook his head. "Even if we just fortified the Nueces and didn't try to defend the Rio Grande crossing, it shifts the advantage too much back to Santa Anna," Will muttered to himself.

"Did you say something, Marse William?" Joe stood in the small doorway. In his hands were Travis' boots.

"My boots." Will silently corrected his thinking, *"No*

*point in thinking of any of this as William B. Travis'
stuff."* He pointed to a spot near the bed and said, "If
you'll put them there I would appreciate it." As Joe set
the boots down, Will glanced up and noticed the slave
couldn't completely hide his ongoing surprise at the
change which had come over his master.

Will made a snap decision as it sunk into his mind
that in every way that it could possibly matter, he was
now William B. Travis. The last remaining doubt that
this was all a dream evaporated in his mind. If that
meant that he now owned the slave, then that meant
that he now had the power to do something about it.
"Joe," he said, "I'm going to have to go fetch Colonel
Fannin shortly. I've seen the way you sit a horse, and
sorry to say, you'd not be able to keep up."

The black man stared back at Will impassively,
remaining quiet. Will's head was spinning as the
remaining words spilled across his lips, "Would you be
willing to fight against Mexico, and when we win our
war, I set you free?"

Joe's impassivity broke and he exclaimed, "Marse
William, you mean to free me if I was to fight for you?"

Will's eyes were shining with his own enthusiasm
when he replied, "Yes or no, Joe. I wouldn't ask it if I
wasn't serious."

A smile slowly crept across Joe's face and he
responded, "Oh, yes sir! I would certainly fight the
Mexicans for my freedom, Marse William."

Joe's smile was infectious and Will couldn't keep one
from his face either. "I thought as much." Will said, "It's
going to take some time to make it official, but I release
you from your bonds now. Whether you fight or not,
Joe, that's up to you. If you choose to fight, then you
will do it as a free man. If you choose to not fight, then

that's also your choice as a free man."

Joe looked a little faint as the news sank in and he sat on the end of the cot as he shook his head, "Lordy, Marse William. I'm free. Does that mean that I can go where I want? If I wanted to go back to Alabama, I could go?"

"It wouldn't be much in the way of freedom if you couldn't. Yes, Joe. You can go wherever you want," Will replied, watching the former slave begin to awaken to the realization of what it could mean to be free. As the smile faded from Joe's face Will noticed a flash of fear replace the smile. Concerned, he said, "Joe, you don't have to make any decisions today about what you want to do. If you want, you can continue to be my servant, but for pay. At least until you know what you want to do."

From the memories of William B. Travis, he had some idea of the next steps. He said, "Joe, I've got to leave now, but when I return, we'll get your manumission forms filed in San Antonio and make it official. You have my word." Will extended his hand, offering it to the former slave. Tentatively Joe reached out and shook his former master's hand, as an equal.

Joining Will on his ride to fetch Fannin was James Butler Bonham. He was a fellow South Carolinian, and if Travis' memories were to be trusted, they were cousins. In addition to their own horses, they each had two more as remounts. Even though he was still sore from sitting in the saddle the previous day, Will set a pace that quickly ate away the miles. At first, Bonham was chatty, talking about various politicians that had assembled at Washington-on-the-Brazos, revealing discord between

Houston and President Burnet over command of Texas military forces, but as the miles fell away, Will's ability to listen to his traveling companion ebbed and when the South Carolinian ran out of steam, he changed the subject, "Jim, have you given much thought about how narrow we're going to cut things?"

Bonham shrugged, and replied, "I'm just a lowly Captain, Buck. I thought they paid you to do the thinking."

Bonham's good humor was contagious, and Will retorted, "Who said anything about getting paid? Sam paying you sub-rosa, Jim?" Both men laughed, but as their horses' hooves kicked up dust, Will mentioned what was on his mind, "Today's Wednesday, the third. We've got what? Ninety miles between here and Goliad, right?"

Bonham nodded, "Sure, how hard do you plan on pushing our horses? That's going to be the difference between two or three days to get there."

Will nodded in response and said, "Right. I don't think we're going to get to Goliad until Friday. How fast we push will decide whether it's in the morning or evening. Let's assume we can get Fannin's men on the march on the sixth. That only gives us nine days to march them over two hundred miles."

Bonham whistled appreciatively, "That means that we're going to need to cover nearly twenty-five miles each day."

"Yeah. That's what I was thinking, too," Will replied. As the two continued in silence for a bit, Will thought about the challenge ahead of him. He knew that the typical infantry force of nineteenth century rarely marched even twenty miles a day. As he thought about it, it triggered something in Will's mind about a story he read about Stonewall Jackson's brigade during the Civil War. In it they covered fifty-seven miles in less than fifty-one hours. Will shook his head, and thought, "Even Stonewall Jackson's famed foot cavalry didn't manage much more than twenty-five miles a day. Were the men with Fannin even capable of that kind of a march, all day, every day for more than a week?" That meant pushing the men for ten hours each day, over nine days. As part of an infantry unit before, finding himself inside of Travis' head, he knew it was physically possible to do it, but he worried that it may stretch Fannin's little army beyond any usefulness. Will despaired at the thought, then despaired even more at the thought of letting Santa Anna march unmolested between the Rio Grande and the Alamo. Unbidden, a single thought lifted his spirits and a burst of laughter escaped his lips. "The difficult we do immediately. The impossible takes a little bit longer," he said as he edged his mount into a gallop. If this impossible takes a little longer, then he knew they had no time to waste. Bonham followed his cousin and spurred his horse down the road.

Pushing through the early February twilight, they slowed down from their earlier steady pace. Will readjusted his backside in the saddle as he marveled at how people in the nineteenth century handled such rigors. The sky was clear and a large yellow moon shone in the night sky when Bonham finally said, "Buck, it's getting late, the road is hard to see, and dammit, my ass is killing me. I don't know how you manage to be stay in the saddle all day long.

Happy to climb down from the horse, Will smirked, thinking that maybe they were so tough because nobody wanted to admit how badly certain body parts hurt. After rubbing down their horses and staking them nearby, Bonham asked, "Do you reckon we made it any further than thirty miles today?" He took a twig and used the small fire they shared to light it before transferring the flame to a cigar.

Will thought about it and said, "Maybe. We left out in the early afternoon. We've been on the road for more than six hours. I guess it's possible." Will calculated the remaining distance and said, "We'll be doing well if we can get there by midafternoon on the 5th. One thing that I am sure about, though, Jim, I'm exhausted."

Bonham agreed and said, "Best then that we get a good night's rest."

Will was satisfied with the time that he and Bonham had made when the two men saw the presidio's white adobe dome gleaming in the noonday sun on the 5th. They had done slightly better than he expected. As they had ridden along the road, Will realized that Bonham enjoyed talking. A lot. He learned that Travis' cousin had come to Texas only a few months prior as part of a militia company from Alabama, called the Mobile Greys. He tuned the other officer out, nodding and grunting responses intermittently.

As they approached the presidio's gate, Will was surprised to see very little activity around its walls. Two men, dressed in the sturdy, gray jackets of the Mobile Greys, stood at what Will generously considered attention. One of the men waved as Will and Bonham arrived, "Howdy, Captain Bonham. I thought you was at the Alamo."

Bonham pulled up in front of the guard and returned the wave with his own casual salute, "Well, Private

Cunningham, here I am, along with Colonel Travis. Where's everyone else? We thought we'd find Colonel Fannin here at Goliad."

The private pulled at the collar of a plain gray jacket, reacting to the chill in the north wind, and replied, "Nah, he and near about everyone else is down Refugio way. They was supposed to meet up with Colonel Grant. Last I heard they hadn't."

Will's stomach felt like it contracted as he felt a sinking feeling. He had been certain that Fannin's force was in Goliad. After all, that's what he remembered from his history books. How could he have been wrong? Doubt crept into his mind. Will swore under his breath and thought, "*If I was wrong about this, what else am I going to be wrong about?*"

Bonham had dismounted and led the horses over to a wooden water trough. "Well, Buck, it doesn't look like we're done for the day. If we hurry along we might be able to get there before it gets dark."

Will woodenly nodded. As he walked around while the horses were drinking from the trough he felt his heart racing, as he worried and wondered about what he thought he knew. He couldn't afford another mistake like this, he thought. "I can't afford to seize up. Too much is riding on not screwing this up." Will thought, "Okay, what do I know about Refugio?" Travis' memories filled in the gaps. The village was less than thirty miles from Goliad.

Bonham came back a few minutes later, pulling a string of four horses. Seeing Will, he cried out, "Good news, Buck. I was able to trade out our tired nags for some fresh mounts."

Hearing Bonham calling out with good news lifted Will's spirits. "Jim, that's well played. Can you find out how many men are still here?" Will asked.

Bonham replied, "Fannin left sixty men to hold the presidio. He's got around three hundred or so with him at the moment."

Feeling better about the news, Will went over to the fresh horses and said, "Jim, would you call all of the men together, we're not going to wait until we meet up with Colonel Fannin to start collecting our army!"

Bonham threw back his head and laughed, "Yes, sir!" Will smiled back and said, "And the impossible, it only takes a little longer."

The sixty men from the presidio followed at a slower pace, afoot, while Will and Bonham rode ahead. When the two rode into Refugio, night had fallen. The campfires dotting the landscape made it apparent to Will that tents, bivouacs, and lean-tos were scattered beyond the village's boundaries. As they rode through the camp, he leaned across to Bonham and asked, "Did we miss the pickets, Jim?"

Bonham shrugged and replied, "I hope so, Buck. What is Jim Fannin up to here?" On the edge of the village stood an adobe house around which several campfires burned. Men in frock coats, homespun, buckskins, and the gray jackets of the New Orleans Greys, lounged about fires. A long string of horses was stabled behind the house. Bonham pointed and said, "I bet we'll find our answers over there."

Bonham previously served with the men from Mobile and several men looked up and waved in recognition when they saw him and Will. As they dismounted, Will quietly said to Bonham, "Jim, go with whatever I say. I have a plan."

Will strode into the small adobe house that Fannin earlier appropriated as his headquarters, with Bonham following on his heels. They found James Fannin sitting near the hearth in a rickety, wooden chair while several other officers lounged around the room. A clay jug of what Will guessed to be mescal was open on large sturdy wooden table. Empty shot glasses surrounded the jug.

It was time to run with an idea that he had been contemplating since he dismounted. Will drew upon the experience of his years in the army and national guard as he came to a ramrod straight attention and threw a parade ground salute to Fannin. He was out of time. In a split second's decision Will knew what he must do. He exclaimed, "Damn it all to hell, Colonel Fannin! I've been looking for you since yesterday."

James Fannin, a tall man with dark brown hair and side whiskers stood and returned the salute, with the precision of a West Point graduate, "To what do I owe the pleasure, Colonel Travis?"

Relaxing a bit, Will reached out and shook Fannin's hand and with as sober an expression as he could manage said, "Last week several families arrived in San Antonio from Coahuila with reliable news. The tyrant himself, Santa Anna is putting down the rebellion in Coahuila and will be marching north within the week. We're in possession of intelligence about his line of march." Bonham cocked an eyebrow at Will but remained silent.

Fannin blanched at the news, his face sagging. "How much time do we have, Colonel Travis? We've got to let Colonel Grant know!"

Will continued wearing a solemn expression when he replied, "We have scant time to react, Colonel

Fannin. Where is Grant?"

"When we last heard from him, his command was waiting at San Patricio," Fannin said, "They were waiting for word from the Coahuilan Federalists that the Centralists have been defeated."

Will looked intently at Fannin, "Jim, did you hear me? there's no time. Colonel Neill and Jim Bowie are moving south to the Rio Grande with most of the artillery from the Alamo. We have just enough time to set up an ambush for Mr. Napoleon of the West!"

Fannin looked stunned, "But how can we abandon Grant, Colonel Travis, we just can't!"

Between the disorganized camp, the lack of guards, and Fannin's indecisiveness, Will was beginning to appreciate why many historians agreed that James Fannin wasn't capable of general command. "Dammit Jim, we're not going to abandon Colonel Grant. We'll sweep by Grant's men at San Patricio on our way to rendezvous with Neill and Bowie. I'm not going to let any of us be left to the tender mercies of Santa Anna's lancers!"

To Will, Fannin looked like some deer caught by the headlights of a car. His mouth opened and closed but no words escaped. Will shook his head, *"No wonder Fannin lost his entire command. The dithering idiot can't make a decision."* It struck him how Fannin's indecision would have cost so many lives, and Will could barely contain his anger, it simmered below the surface when he said, "Jim. I know you were appointed colonel of the army to invade Matamoros, but, good God man, will you consent to be my second-in-command for the good of the revolution?"

Will shocked himself by his own audacity. However, everyone else in the room stared slack-jawed at Will's daring. Will knew as a student of history, in the Revolution, the Texians had allowed their shared goals to be undermined by clashes of egos. What Will didn't know was how few men were willing to risk a breach of honor to cause a duel. Bonham stepped up behind his cousin and friend, a sign of support that wasn't lost on the other men in the room. The weight of command that had been an incredible burden to James Fannin suddenly became light as a feather as he returned Will's gaze with a look of gratefulness. He stood from the wooden chair and saluted, "Colonel Travis, we are at your command!"

Will grinned, ignorant of the deadly game of honor that he had won. "Let's fill these glasses, gentlemen!" he said, gesturing to the empty shot glasses on the table. Colonel Fannin grabbed the jug of mescal. He poured generous amounts in each of the glasses and passed them around to everyone in the room. Feeling a deep sense of relief, they lifted their glasses in a toast. Bonham nodded to Will, and exclaimed, "To our friend and commander, Colonel Travis!" Will smiled at the toast, and took a long sip of the rough mescal, before responding, "No, my friends. Santa Anna considers himself the Napoleon of the West. I do not fancy myself to be his Wellington, but my friends, one thing is sure. We shall make him meet his Waterloo. To his Waterloo!"

Chapter 5

The first sign Will was awake was his throbbing mescal-induced hangover. He painfully opened one of his eyes and watched a narrow ray of light work its way across the floor as it filtered through a window into the cramped adobe house. Next, the odor of unwashed bodies wafted into his nose. Hangover or no, he had to get out of the cramped quarters. He stumbled to his feet and kicked at Bonham's leg and in a scratchy voice said, "Jim. You alive?"

From beneath a multicolored Mexican horse blanket, he heard Bonham's muffled voice, "No."

Will kicked a little harder, and watched the other man jerk his leg away. Will sighed as a sharp pain behind his eye made him wince. He rubbed his forehead, and said, "Come on Jim, we're burning daylight."

As he cracked the door open and slid out, Will saw a few men fixing breakfast around a campfire and stumbled over and asked, "Any of you boys spare a cup of coffee?"

One of the men found a banged up tin cup amid a

small pile of tinware, drying on a small, square tarpaulin. After accepting the hot tin cup from the soldier, Will edged up closer to the fire, lifted the cup to his face, and breathed in the brew's strong aroma. He looked at the man that handed him coffee and asked, "Where abouts are y'all from?"

The man replied, "We're from Georgia. Us boys are part of Ward's battalion, sir." Will recalled from history that Ward's Georgians made up the largest part of Fannin's small army in his own recollection of history. He thanked the soldier for the coffee and sauntered through the camp. Dozens of campfires were rekindled as the soldiers rose to face the chilly day. The entire camp seemed to know that Will and Bonham's arrival signaled a new direction. He eventually found a spot near the adobe house where he sat on a mesquite stump, watching several men as they cleaned their rifles and muskets. Another was darning a hole in his sock, while several others folded up a tent. Will glanced into the rapidly brightening sky, and noticed that the effects of his hangover were fading as the caffeine kicked in. The morning was getting away from him, he realized. As he had told Bonham earlier, they were burning daylight.

When Fannin's two small battalions were drawn up in long lines outside of the little village, the sun was well into the sky on the morning of the 6th of February. Will sat atop his horse and looked across the field where the little army assembled. It reminded him of the day the 144th Infantry was deployed from Fort Hood to Iraq over eight months previously. It was a study in contrasts. He remembered the six hundred national guardsmen and women standing at attention on the parade ground dressed sharply in their BDUs. They stood in stark contrast from the men assembled on the windswept prairie.

His National Guard unit was a melting pot of people from every culture in Texas, white, brown, and black faces. and every shade in between. These men were nearly uniformly white, with a few Tejano faces in the mix. They were garbed in every conceivable dress common to the American frontier. A few men wore old, blue army jackets, a few from Georgia wore the gray jackets that they had received from the militia armories. Those from the New Orleans Greys wore sturdy gray jackets that were uniform in their workmanlike design. Among the rest, there were men in frock coats, hunting shirts and buckskin jackets. In an age of muskets, many of the men carried their carefully tended hunting rifles, while others were armed with muskets and even shotguns. Despite the contrast between these men and those of the 144th Infantry, he saw in them the same dogged determination that he had seen on a dozen missions in Iraq. More than that, Will realized, these men were looking to him to lead them to victory.

He forced down the burden of weighty responsibility that he felt as he watched the 350 men standing along a front that stretched over a hundred yards. He found it breathtaking. Nodding to Fannin, Will said, "Give the command. Daylight's burning."

Will had sent the three field guns on ahead earlier that morning, moving south, toward Refugio, with an hour's head start. Most of the excess horses were detailed to accompany the artillery. He thought that if the horses could be rotated out, the artillery may stay up with the infantry and not slow them down. Will was acutely aware that Fannin's trials with his artillery were some of the myriad of problems that overwhelmed the ineffectual colonel in the history he knew.

As the column started down the road to Refugio, Will sought the captain of their mounted rifles, a tall, black-haired man named Albert Horton. Captain Horton saluted when Will rode up. Will said, "Captain, I'd like for you to divide your company into two parts. I want you to set half your men here, covering our flanks, and take the other half and scout ahead of our artillery."

Horton nodded thoughtfully at the command and said, "Yes, sir, Colonel Travis." He wheeled about and raced to put the order into action. Throughout the day, Will worked with Fannin and Ward to halt the column every hour for ten minutes, allowing his force to rest while still making good time along the coastal road to Refugio. Also, he sent orders back to the sixty men who were marching behind them. Will thought it likely those men would remain a day's march behind the column for a while.

The chill February sun had been gone from the western sky for more than an hour when Will's column of infantry trudged into Refugio. Earlier in the evening, as the sun was going down, Horton's advanced scouts had entered Refugio and notified Colonel Grant that Colonels Travis and Fannin would arrive that evening.

Will's men entered Refugio and saw that Grant had turned out his entire command, lining the road with his men, as they cheered the arrival of the small army. Will was taken a little by surprise at the impromptu welcome. As he, Bonham, Fannin, and Ward rode into the little hamlet, they were escorted to an adobe hut even smaller than the one Fannin had used in Goliad. Colonel James Grant greeted them at the door.

He waved Will and the others to enter, and in a thick Scottish brogue, Grant addressed Fannin, "I would ne'er have expected to see you here again Jim, after ye let

Houston talk ye into giving up on Matamoros. What changed your mind?"

Will turned to Ward and asked, "Colonel Ward, kindly see to the men's wellbeing this evening."

Ward looked relieved as he glanced in the tiny hut that was crowded before Will entered. With a hint of a smile he replied, "Yes, sir."

Will entered the one-room cabin and immediately felt claustrophobic. Fannin and Bonham were crowded around a table with Grant and another man, whom Will presumed was Frank Johnson. As Will joined them at the table, Fannin responded to Grant's earlier jibe. "Well, things change, James. Colonel Travis here has received word that Santa Anna is already marching through Coahuila with a large force."

Grant started to reply to Fannin when Will took that moment to interject, "Colonel Grant, I want you to be aware that Colonels Neill and Bowie are staging a force of artillery and riflemen at the Rio Grande, where the Camino Real intersects it. Every man who owes allegiance to Texas is needed to reinforce them. We have a unique opportunity to stop Santa Anna and his army dead in their tracks before they can even cross into Texas!"

Grant's words died on his lips as he heard Will's impassioned plea. Will could see that Grant was torn between what he wanted to do, which likely included rushing pell-mell to Matamoros, and where momentum was building. Grant grew thoughtful for a moment. "Do ye think that after we repulse Santa Anna's Centralist forces there that you'd join us in liberating the remainder of *Tejas y Coahuila*?" Will was momentarily puzzled about Grant's request, but Travis' memories came to the rescue, once again. He recalled the Texas

Revolution was one of several revolts against Santa Anna's Centralist government about the same time. Ultimately, it was the most successful. With an inkling that Grant's concern was more about his large landholding south of the Rio Grande, Will decided a neutral response was safest. "Let's fight one battle at a time Colonel Grant. If God sees fit to grant us success, well then, we'll gather round the victory fires and see if what you propose is feasible."

It was clear to Will and the other officers in the room that Grant was disappointed, but even so, he smiled feebly and replied, "Fair enough."

The next morning, the 7th of February, dawned as clear and cold as the day before. The artillery with their mounted escort leading the way had rolled out, heading west as the eastern sky grew light in early morning. With Grant's force rolled into his own, Will now commanded more than 450 men. There was no comparing his life within the 144th Infantry against what he encountered now. It was simply too alien to reconcile the two experiences. Keeping that in his mind, he felt a thrill of adventure as he galloped to the head of the column of marching men.

Four years active duty and three more in the guard, left Will thinking that he was in excellent shape, but after nine days of endless marching he and every one of his men were bone-tired and dirty. They marched along the Camino Real and watched as the wide muddy expanse, known by the Texians as the Rio Grande, and by the Mexicans as *El Rio Bravo del Norte* came into view. Above the smell of stale sweat, the light breeze carried a whiff of decaying vegetation along the bank of the river. He turned around in the saddle, noticing that after so many days in it, either his butt muscles had strengthened or he was too numb to care. He saw his column of infantry strung out, doggedly marching along the Camino Real toward the river. Despite the unforgiving terrain and cold weather, almost the entire command was behind him. Less than a score of men had fallen out or quit the forced march. Also, to his complete surprise, the previous evening, the sixty men from Goliad had caught up with his main force.

As the orange sun sank below the western horizon on that Monday evening the 15th of February, Will led five hundred men into an encampment on the northern bank of the Rio Grande. Dozens of men stopped their work, entrenching the Alamo's field guns into protected earthen embankments, and ran out to cheer as the men in Will's command straightened their jackets and coats, stood a little taller, and marched a little straighter. Within the ranks of the tired, marching men, someone started singing, 'The Girl I Left Behind', and the entire column joined in, swelling in volume fueled by the cheering men from the Alamo.

Turning to Fannin, Will said, "Jim, please dismiss the men. Tell them that they have just done the impossible." From there, Will threaded his horse through the throng of cheering men. He saw Jim Bowie standing next to a once-white dingy tent, several hundred feet from the river. Next to Bowie, he saw Juan Seguin and another tall man with dark-brown hair, wearing a buckskin jacket and brown vest.

As Will climbed down from the saddle, Bowie stepped up and slapped him on the shoulders, exclaiming, "Damned if I know how you did it, but you must have found every Texian west of the Brazos, Buck!" Will grinned as he continued, "Y'all are a beautiful sight to behold."

He noticed that Bowie looked exhausted. Dark circles under his eyes belied his cheerful tone. Will smiled and responded, "You did well yourself, Jim."

He reached out and shook Juan Seguin's hand, and said, "I'm glad to see that you were able to make it, Juan. How many men came with you?"

The swarthy, rail-thin Tejano clasped hands with Will and beamed at him, saying, "I visited many of the haciendas to the south of Bexar and found fifty men who agreed to fight against the tyrant."

The last man looked at Will with piercing brown eyes. Will noticed the straight black hair that flowed over the collar, which belonged to an elaborately beaded buckskin coat. Under the coat was an orange lined doe-skin vest, embroidered with stars. This last man was of a similar height to Will's own frame of six feet. While his face carried a stern countenance, his dark eyes held a twinkle of mischief. From many pictures, Will recognized that he was standing in front of a veritable living legend, the nineteenth century cross between Elvis Presley and California Governor Ronald Reagan, Colonel David Crockett. Will couldn't say if it was from far too many hours in the saddle but he felt more than just a little giddy as Crockett reached out and shook his hand.

In a soft voice, Crockett said, "I finally have the honor of meeting the one and only, 'Buck' Travis. Colonel Bowie speaks highly of you, as did Colonel Neill. And as I live and breathe," he paused as he indicated to the newly arrived soldiers, "you have earned the reputation."

Later that night, Will tried to sleep, but the immensity of becoming Travis settled on him as he thought about Bowie and Crockett. Each was larger than life to a boy who loved Texas history. As a child, when he had visited the Alamo, he had been awed by the bravery and courage that William B. Travis had shown throughout the siege. Bowie's larger than life legend revolved as much around the knife as much as it had the man, but the man had inspired a hundred volunteers to follow him to the Alamo. His place in the pantheon of Texas legends had been earned. But something separated Crockett from the other two. Objectively, Will knew that Travis had owed his fame to commanding the doomed defense, while Bowie was a regional celebrity. Crockett, on the other hand, had cast a shadow of celebrity over the entire nation in the years before the Alamo.

No, Will realized, it wasn't Crockett's national fame which set him apart from Travis or Bowie. Will had been shamed by many of the memories he had inherited from Travis. Even by the standards of the day in which he found himself, by any reasonable standard, Travis had been a deadbeat father and an adulterer. Even now, the ink was barely dry on Travis' divorce papers. His thoughts turned to Bowie, who had made his fortune the previous decade buying and selling slaves. Then there was Crockett. David Crockett was unsullied by the violence that was Bowie's stock-in-trade, and was a faithful family man. His singular sin in the eyes of his contemporaries was picking a fight with President Jackson over the Indian Removal Policy. In Will's eyes, Crockett was very much a hero. As Will drifted off to sleep his mind was filled with images of Crockett swinging his rifle around his head in front of the Alamo

Chapel as Santa Anna's *soldados* overwhelmed him.

As the sun dawned on February 16th, Will awoke to the sound of something sizzling on a nearby fire. He inhaled the fragrant aroma of bacon. He crawled out of his bedroll and found his Bonham balancing a skillet on a rock next to a campfire. A short distance away, under a wide, white tarp, that served duty as the command post, Will saw Bowie and Fannin sitting in narrow camp chairs beside a collapsible camp table. When Bowie saw Will stirring, he called out, "Buck, I've got a pot of coffee here, why don't you join us."

Will settled onto a short camp stool and accepted the steaming cup of black coffee. He hadn't seen Colonel James Neill since arriving and asked about him. Bowie replied, "Colonel Neill didn't make it with us. We were already on the road when he received a message telling him that his family was taken seriously ill. He said that he hoped to meet up with us at the Alamo in a few weeks," Bowie continued, "What are the plans, Buck? You got us all gussied up and ready to dance."

Will had compiled a mental inventory, but thought it best to confirm their assets with the others. He said, "Let's take stock of what we have. With our additional field pieces, what do we have, fifteen cannons?"

Captain Carey joined Bonham at the nearby campfire and turned when he heard Will. He replied, "That's right. We brought all two-hundred loads for them. Just no solid shot or exploding shells."

Will beckoned Carey over to the table, "Where do we stand on having our guns emplaced along the ford here?"

Carey grinned, "Finished last night, Colonel. Each gun has a few loads ready to go, but most of them are well away from our batteries."

Will asked, "Why?"

Carey responded, "Our cannon are shotguns on wheels, sir. Very deadly out to a hundred yards. But when the Mexicans attack, we'll only get one chance to fire the cannon.

"*No surprises there.*" Will thought. He turned to Bowie and asked, "Jim, what's the disposition of our men?"

Bowie said, "Buck, when you left, we had one hundred forty men. We left a dozen to keep an eye on the sick and wounded at the hospital, but even so, we marched out with one hundred twenty-eight men. Seguin here met us at the Nueces with fifty men, and Colonel Crockett with his dozen. So, we've positioned ourselves along the north bank of the Rio Grande, with our cannon dug in, with one hundred ninety men effective for duty."

Will saw Fannin preening, waiting for Bowie to finish talking. He asked, "What about your men, James?"

"Once we scooped up Colonel Grant's men along with our reserves from Goliad, we brought in more than five hundred men, Colonel Travis." Fannin said, "Between Jim's and ours we've got seven hundred here!"

Will and the other officers fell silent in astonishment, realizing they had managed to collect seven hundred men on the banks of the Rio Grande and had done it before Santa Anna's army arrived. As it dawned on them what they had accomplished, everyone smiled. There was only one other thing needed. Defeat Santa Anna.

Chapter 6

Will stood on the north bank of the Rio Grande, along with Colonels Fannin and Bowie, David Crockett, and Captains Seguin, Carey, and Dickinson. He looked across the wide river with a telescoping spyglass. It spanned more than four hundred feet, but south of the ford was a low island that hugged the Texas side of the river for five hundred feet. After talking to Seguin earlier, it was clear that this was the only place where Santa Anna could safely send his artillery across the river within dozens of miles. He turned to Seguin, "Juan, what do we know about other nearby fords?"

Seguin replied, "There's another ford a few miles northeast of a little village of Guerrero over across the river. Other than that, there may be places to ford, but they pose challenges regarding infantry and artillery, as the terrain inconvenient to both."

Will nodded. Seguin's synopsis made sense, but he wanted more information about the ford upriver. "How far away from here is this other ford and what makes this one here better than that one, Juan?"

"The other ford is maybe twenty miles north," Seguin said, "But it's two hundred yards wider and maybe a foot deeper. I have a few men stationed up there, just in case we're wrong."

Will frowned and shook his head. This wasn't an ideal place to do battle given the low rising island that ran south of the ford. Finally, he said, "It's not the most ideal location, gentlemen, but we either stop him here for a while or we hightail it back to the Nueces and try again."

Bowie waved Will's comment away, "When we came

south across the Nueces, it wasn't much more than a lazy creek, Buck. I'm sure we could hold them on the Nueces, but even if that damned island is an inconvenience, I think this is still a better choice for us."

Captain Dickinson added, "Colonel Travis, with your permission, I'd like to show you what we've done with our artillery." Will nodded and he continued, "We've taken the dozen cannon from the Alamo and set them up in four batteries of three guns each, along the river." He paused, and pointed to the north of where they were standing, at an earthen embankment a short distance away. "That's our first one, and it covers the narrow ford from the north."

He pointed at another embankment southeast of where they stood, and said, "The second battery covers the ford from the east. These six guns will provide overlapping fields of fire. The other two batteries are emplaced to stop any troops trying to use the island when crossing the river."

Will looked at the northern head of the island and asked, "Do we know how deep and wide the channel between the island and our side of the river is?"

Captain Carey said, "The channel is one hundred feet wide the length of the island. If Santa Anna tried to put his *cazadores* on the island, that could make things difficult for us. The good news is that the midpoint of the channel is four feet deep or more."

Will grimaced at the thought of his men coming under fire from the Mexican skirmishers. "We'll just have to keep them from doing that. Now how many men do you need on the guns?"

Carey replied, "That depends on what's required." Seeing the confusion on Will's face, he clarified, "Let's keep in mind that without solid shot or explosive shells, our artillery are just giant shotguns, sir. I wouldn't try firing at targets more than a hundred yards away. Almaron and I are of two minds on how to defend the river crossing. First, I am of the opinion that we have a single opportunity to stop an attack. And we're not likely to get a second chance to fire the cannons. Without solid shot, all we can do is use them for canister. I'm concerned that even with a crew of six men for each gun we'd be pressing them to do more than a round in a minute. If we can get one good volley with them, it may be the best that we can do. It could be different if our crews were well trained, but most of them are doing well to know how to swab the barrel. Now, if this scenario comes to pass, then we really only need two men per cannon on the batteries covering the ford. On the other hand, we can't predict what the Mexicans are going to do with the island. I would recommend that on batteries covering it, that we assign a full complement of six men per cannon."

Will nodded thoughtfully. Carey's reasoning made sense, but he wanted to hear Captain Dickinson's thoughts, too. "Almaron, where do you differ with William?"

Dickinson said, "We can't know for certain what will happen at the ford. Bill's right that if we only have one chance, then a full crew of men is wasted. But if things go differently, then a full crew would allow us to keep these guns in action, beyond just a single volley."

Even though the two officers were in disagreement on tactics, Will was pleased they were both thinking through their roles in the coming fight. When he thought back on his own previous experience with combat, he knew just how chaotic and fast changing a situation could become. The odds that they could reload their guns on the ford were slim. Will addressed the two artillerists. "Those are both good points. However, I tend to agree with Captain Carey. Captain Dickinson, you'll be in command of the batteries facing the island, and Carey, you'll take the other two. I'd suggest that y'all go pick your men."

Once the two artillery officers left, he turned to the remaining officers, "Next we need to decide how to deploy our infantry."

At that point, Crockett, who had been quietly observing the conversation, interjected, "Colonel Travis, if I might, I'd like to discuss an idea about our infantry. Do we know how many rifles we have? They've got a sight longer range than our smoothbore muskets."

After several minutes of discussion, they determined that there were approximate 350 rifles among the seven hundred men. The rest were armed with muskets and shotguns. Crockett continued, "Colonel, back when I served under Andy Jackson, you could take three hundred men with muskets, put 'em in a line and at one hundred yards, maybe twenty or thirty might hit their target, maybe. But I know of riflemen that could knock the flea off a mule's ass at two hundred yards every time. Imagine if we took our best one hundred twenty riflemen and placed them along the ford here, then take another two men and assign them to each shooter as reloaders. Would you agree that each shooter should be able to fire six aimed shots per minute if he had two men to reload for him?"

Will chuckled in appreciation. He'd wondered how best to position his little army at the ford since arriving the previous evening. As an experienced rifleman himself, Will was bemused that he hadn't thought of this solution himself. "That's an excellent idea. You figure those men would be able to send over seven hundred aimed shots into a Mexican attack in the first minute?"

Crockett nodded, "Near 'nuff. If we can't put a serious hurt into Santa Anna's plans, then I'm not Davy Crockett, Lion of the West!" He theatrically puffed out his chest, grabbed his buckskin jacket by the lapels and flashed a toothy grin at the other officers.

Bowie slapped him on the back, laughing and asked, "You been riding any lightnin' bolts lately Davy?"

Crockett ruefully chuckled and grew somber before saying, "I don't know what I was thinking, letting that damn fool writer, Paulding, take some of my better stories and make that silly play. But that palaver earned me that last term in Congress. I must say I enjoyed tremendously yanking ol' Andy Jackson's tail more than once while I was there."

"Unless anyone has an objection, once we're done, Colonel Crockett, why don't you work with Fannin and Bowie here to find your sharpshooters."

Crockett quickly replied, "Oh, Colonel Buck, I'm just a high private. I ain't been a colonel since my neighbors back in Tennessee elected me. And they only did that because I brought more corn liquor to the muster than the fellow I ran against."

Will flashed Crockett a malicious grin and replied, "Does anyone other than *Colonel* Crockett have any objections?"

After everyone, including Crockett, laughed at his expense, Will circled back around to their defense. "We've assigned fifty men to the artillery and *Colonel* Crockett's got another three hundred sixty men. That leaves us with just under three hundred men to assign." Will turned to Fannin and said, "James, I want you to take your Georgia and Lafayette battalions, less any riflemen, and dig in along the river facing the island. Between Dickinson's artillery and your infantry, you should be able to deny the Mexicans use of the island."

After Fannin acknowledged the order, Will turned to Bowie and Seguin and said, "The two of you, and your men, are our reserve command. Juan, once the action starts, take your company to our southern or left flank and if the Mexicans try to flank us there, stop them. Jim," Will said to Bowie, "After Crockett gets his riflemen, I want you to take your remaining volunteers to our right flank, and keep the Mexicans from flanking us to our north. Does anyone have any questions?"

As the other officers left to take care of their responsibilities, Will placed his hand on the Tennessean's shoulder and said, "Congressman Crockett, I hope you don't mind the responsibility. I know that you weren't looking for command. But I also have confidence in your ability, else I'd not ask this."

Crockett shrugged his shoulders and smiled wistfully, "Call me David, please. I got no problem leading these boys. But I'm mindful that they're going to remember me a lot more fondly if they see I'm one of them, not some highfalutin officer, telling them what to do."

Will returned the smile, "We all like to be led from the front, I think. Do you reckon that there's enough cover along our side of the river for your boys to fire from protected positions?"

Crockett scanned the sides of the road that ended at the river's edge and replied, "With enough time I can set most of our teams in their own protected shooting blinds."

As Crockett walked toward a group of men with hunting rifles, Will strode back toward the encampment, a few hundred feet from the water's edge and found Bonham resting on the smelly Mexican horse blanket he had taken from Fannin's headquarters in Refugio.

"Fancy a little exercise, Jim?" Will asked.

Bonham rolled over, crinkling his nose at the pungent odor of the blanket and replied, "What have you got in mind, Buck?"

"Let's you and me go check out the other side of the river," Will replied.

Bonham's eyes lit up like a firework show as he jumped to his feet, "What are you waiting for?"

Will went back to the ford, while Bonham saddled his horse. While he waited for his cousin, he watched Crockett work with a team of three men as they arranged a fallen log and scrub brush into a concealed location. Several dozen more teams were collecting brush, branches and whatever driftwood was available into their own hunting blinds. To the south, at the nearest battery he saw Captain Dickinson sighting one of the cannons at a spot in the middle of the river. He smiled. These were good men.

Bonham trotted up a short while later, armed with his own shotgun, "Shall we go visit old Mexico, Buck?"

Their horses splashed into the shallows of the ford and they edged them through the frigid, fast flowing water. About midway across the river, Will guessed the water was less than three feet deep. He could see why the Camino Real came this route. Nearing the south bank of the river, the water became shallower until the horses stamped their hooves on dry ground.

Will noted that the southern bank of the Rio Grande was like the northern, although to him, it seemed like there were more prickly pear cacti growing near the river's southern edge. Mesquite trees grew next to the cacti lining the road leading away from the river, angling to the southwest. Will leaned over and nudged Bonham, "That's likely where they'll be coming. Shall we scout down it a bit?"

They rode their mounts down the narrow track, where ruts from heavy wagons had scarred the roadbed. At several places branches from mesquite trees edged into the road, causing the two riders to swing wide around the thorny branches. After avoiding a mesquite branch's sharp thorns, Will looked up and saw in the distance a cloud of dust to their south. He said, "James, look ahead."

As Bonham's eyes followed Will's finger, to the dust cloud in the distance, Will looked down the winding dirt road and saw a flash of metal in the late morning sun. He pointed it out to Bonham and said, "I guess we know where Santa Anna's army is. Let's get on back across the river."

They turned to leave, and as their horses started back toward the river, Bonham's mount stepped into a rut, and stumbled. Will heard a loud snapping sound and watched his cousin react to his horse falling into the road. Bonham leapt free a second before his leg would have been crushed under the fallen animal. He climbed back to his feet, his jacket covered in grayish brown dust. As the horse lay on the road, Will saw the twisted angle of the front right leg, and knew this was bad. Bonham swore until he noticed the leg then swore again as he glanced behind him and saw the glint of sunlight reflecting off an upraised lance. A few hundred yards away, both men could see a couple of Mexican lancers emerge around a bend in the road. "Jim," Will urged, "take my hand!"

Bonham looked down at his horse and swore yet again as he worked his shotgun loose from the scabbard, beneath the fallen mount. He took Will's outstretched arm and flung himself up behind his cousin. As Bonham grabbed him around the waist, Will dug his heels into his horse as they navigated the poorly maintained wagon road. As they hurried back toward to the river the injured horse's neighing faded away, washed out by the sound of hoofs clattering down the road behind them.

As he and Bonham emerged from the road, dust billowing behind them, Will guided his horse back into the frigid, flowing river. Behind them he heard shouts and the sound of horses clopping along the road. Will caught the distinct sound of Bonham's shotgun cocking. He had guided the horse less than a quarter of the way across the river when he chanced a look around and saw two Mexican lancers emerge from the mesquite-lined road behind them. He urged the horse further into the river, and felt Bonham bring the shotgun to his shoulder and involuntarily ducked when he heard the flint strike the firing pan. The gun boomed and he felt Bonham push into him with the gun's recoil. Will's ears were ringing; otherwise he would have heard a body splashing into the river.

As the ringing in his ears faded, Will felt his horse's shoes land in the soft dirt on the north bank of the river. After Bonham slid down from behind him he wheeled around and saw the two lancers who had pursued them. One was dismounted, dragging his companion from the water. He watched long enough to see several dozen more lancers spread out along the banks as they flowed from the road. Flashes of sunlight glinted off their shiny metal helmets and the tips of their long, deadly lances.

The leading elements of the Dolores Cavalry Regiment made a fine spectacle on the south bank of the Rio Grande, in their blue and red uniforms. Several soldiers edged into the water, before being called back by their officers. Will watched an elaborately dressed officer, perhaps the company commander, peering across the river, studying the nearby earthen gun emplacements. He wondered what was going through the mind of the Mexican officer when he realized that any effort to cross the river would only be won with the shedding of blood.

Chapter 7

Will stared back at the officer on the opposite bank and wondered what the Mexican officer saw from his view. When he and Bonham returned a few minutes before, they had been preoccupied by what was behind them than by what was in front of them. "What does he think of the two batteries that are visible?" Will asked. Looking around, Will could see telltale signs of several of Crockett's blinds, but could scarcely imagine what they looked like from the other side of the river.

Over the next half hour, Will watched from one of the rifle blinds the balance of the Dolores Cavalry Regiment assembled on the Mexican side of the Rio Grande. By walking along behind the rifle blinds, he found Crockett with a couple of other riflemen. He slid down next to Crockett behind the fallen log and said, "You ready, David?"

Crockett kept his eyes focused across the river, "Near 'nuff, Colonel Buck. Do wish that whoever put this road here had chosen a wider section of the river. Heard tell it was a mile wide and foot deep. Somebody's been telling tales out of school 'bout this river." Will chuckled at Crockett's witty reply, until he continued, "Those lancers are outside of effective musket range, but at two hundred yards, well, we could stop with them with our rifles from sitting there pretty on their horses, if you wanted."

Will shook his head, "No. We'll catch them when they cross. Let their lead elements get about a third of the way across then give them a big Texas howdy."

They watched the lancers form up, twenty men across, perhaps the width of a platoon, to keep to the shallows of the ford. As soon as the lancers were in position, the officer in a fancy uniform stored his spyglass and rode over to the first line of lancers. He pulled a sword, that reflected the noonday sun and waved it in the direction of the Texas side of the river. As the first line of lancers trotted forward, Will heard a high melodic note from a bugle float across the river, announcing the start of the battle of the Rio Grande.

As the leading line of lancers splashed into the fast flowing, frigid water, Will noticed that amid the prickly pear cactus and the dense mesquite trees on the Mexican side, several men, dressed in blue jackets and white pants, were afoot on both sides of the road. The forward elements of Santa Anna's infantry had arrived. Will's attention came back to the lancers. The first row of riders approached Crockett's imagined mark mid-river. He watched the Tennessean, with the gunstock firmly pressed into his shoulder, cock the flintlock and sight down the barrel. A moment later, he fired and Will's eyes flew back to the charging cavalry. The dandily dressed officer flung his hands out, and somersaulted off the back of his horse, sinking beneath the flowing water.

Crockett's rifle shot signaled the Texians' response

to the charging cavalry. More than a hundred rifles discharged their deadly projectiles, lashing out at the advancing lancers who were less than halfway across the river. Save for one lancer in the first rank, all the others were knocked from their saddles by accurate fire from the hidden riflemen. Several horses were hit and floundered helplessly in mid-river.

Crockett handed the empty rifle to one of his reloaders, took the proffered loaded rifle and brought it up to his shoulder where a moment later he fired again. Dozens of more rifles spit out death at the charging lancers.

From the Mexican line a bugle sounded an urgent tattoo and the Lancers still mounted surged forward, through the middle of the river, the water coming up to their horses' bellies. With the third rifle, Crockett aimed at the nearest lancer, several horse-lengths ahead of his nearest companion, yet more than fifty yards from the Texas shoreline. With a ringing boom, a lead ball exploded from the barrel of Crockett's rifle, the lancer dropped his weapon and clutched his right shoulder. A second later another bullet from a different sharpshooter dismounted the injured man.

Dozens of riderless horses milled around in the middle of the river, bumping against the bodies drifting away downstream. As Crockett and his two reloaders hurried to reload their rifles, Will watched the lancers in the rearmost line jerking their reins and pushing their horses back to southern side of the river. The balance of the surviving lancers wheeled around and navigated around panicked horses and bodies of their fellow cavalrymen bobbing in the water until they reached the relative safety of the shoreline.

Will stared at the carnage floating and floundering in

the river. Bodies of man and beast drifted along with the current, tinging the river with wide swaths of red. Closing his eyes at that moment Will was years and miles away. He was in Fallujah, Iraq, 2004, he crouched behind a wrecked, white Nissan subcompact car. He peeked through the shattered passenger-side window, looking for the sniper, who had sent him scurrying for cover. Several other men from his squad were nearby. He heard Corporal White screaming. The sniper had shot him in the leg. The rest of the squad was searching for him.

Will scanned a low-rise apartment building opposite from the wrecked car and thought he saw a glint of something. He wondered if it could it be the scope from the sniper's rifle. As he stared at the spot, he watched a rifle barrel extend from the window then the outline of shooter's head. He bit back laughter. He had expected the head to be wrapped in a turban, but instead, he saw a baseball cap turned around backward. He pushed the absurd thought away and sighted his service rifle through the shattered window of the Nissan. He felt his hands shaking as he tried to line the baseball cap in his sights. He took a deep breath and mentally said the first line of the Lord's Prayer. It struck him as irreverent, but it helped to steel his nerves and steady his aim. He looked back through the rifle's sight and saw the baseball-capped sniper. Will squeezed the trigger and felt the recoil slam into his shoulder. A puff of red and gray mist filled the center of his sights. He lowered his rifle and watched the sniper pitch forward out the window, as he somersaulted and fell into a fountain in the apartment's courtyard.

The baseball cap floated in the water, as the sniper's body bobbed facedown. The water in the fountain turned a deep shade of pink. Will snapped back to the present and felt the memory recede as he focused on the bodies slipping downstream.

As the last of the lancers splashed ashore amid a flurry of rifle fire, Crockett called out, "That's enough, boys. I think they know we're here now."

From the blind, Will watched as the remaining officers and NCOs restored order to the unit. Riderless horses trotted onto both sides of the river as well as onto the narrow island below the ford, many of their riders lost to the currents of the ever-flowing Rio Grande. Two hundred ninety men rode into the waters of the Rio Grande to punish the upstart Texians, but less than two hundred returned to the shore. Many of the wounded had drowned before they could be rescued from the fast-flowing waters of the Rio Grande.

When the sun descended into the western sky, Will saw three different regimental standards set back from the banks of the river and a larger flag of the Mexican Republic flying further back. As Will slid down the earthen embankment at Captain Carey's battery, he saw Bowie approaching. The knife fighter pointed to the distant pendant and said, "That big flag, flying over yonder, that's *el presidente* himself, Buck."

Will gestured toward the regimental standards and asked, "Do you know anything about those regiments over there?" as he handed over the spyglass.

Bowie looked through the telescoping lens before saying, "two of them are part of Santa Anna's regular army. I see the standards for the Jiménez Regiment as well as the Matamoros Regiment. I'm not familiar with the third regiment, but judging by their uniforms, I think they belong to the active militia."

Will thought back to what he remembered of the

Alamo, and something triggered. The reason that Santa Anna allowed the siege to go on for thirteen days was because his army was strung out over more than a hundred miles at the start of the siege. Could he be so lucky that Santa Anna would attempt to storm across the Rio Grande with this lone brigade at his immediate disposal?

Bowie pointed across the river, "Look at that, Buck. It appears that Santa Anna's got his dander up. Could it be he's going to make another attempt?"

Sure enough, men were filtering through the mesquite trees, funneling onto the shoreline, where they were densely packed. Will's lips skinned back in a vicious grin as with great fanfare, bugles and drums began pounding out a martial tune. Bowie, still standing beside him, pointed at the nearest regimental flag, "It looks like he's going to send the Jiménez Regiment across first."

The second regiment, Matamoros, crowded behind them, while Will could see the white uniforms of the militia still assembling in the mesquite trees.

As best as he could tell, the two regular regiments were deployed in lines three men deep. Somewhere in the back of his mind, this registered as a formation common during the Napoleonic wars. It appeared the two leading regiments had no more than three hundred men each and the militia regiment that followed behind them appeared to have less than five hundred men.

Along a front of nearly a hundred men, as best as Will could estimate, the first regiment splashed into the river. If Santa Anna wanted another fight, then Will was determined to give it to him. He saw Captain Carey standing next to a 6-pounder and he yelled, "Carey! If they get within forty yards, give them hell!"

Will sprinted from the battery back over to Crockett's blind, skidding into it. The frontiersman looked up and said, "Come to watch the fun, Colonel Buck?"

Will grinned sheepishly as he plucked a few twigs from his uniform. "David, whenever you're ready." Like before, Will watched Crockett go to work at his craft as the cramped Mexican line pushed through the water cresting their knees and calves. Crockett's rifle shot signaled his sharpshooters, and they opened a devastating fire on the advancing men of the Jiménez Regiment. The first volley from Crockett's riflemen felled dozens of men in the front rank of the Mexican line regiment. But the men in the second rank quickly stepped forward as they continued slogging through the water, that came to their waists. After firing a second round, Crockett handed the rifle to one of the reloaders and shouted to Will, "Going to check on the rest of the boys. Be right back."

Despite his years of experience as a soldier and guardsman, Will was in awe as he watched Crockett walk along behind the line of blinds shouting encouragement to the riflemen and steadying frayed nerves. Crockett's earlier words about leading from the front rather than pushing from the rear came back to Will and he knew that Crockett's action was not simply right for the old Indian fighter but a lesson for himself. Will leapt up, drew his sword and rushed to the opposite side of the road, where half the blinds were set up. From his new vantage point, Will could see many of the riflemen firing their weapons and taking a loaded gun from one of the reloaders.

Will trained his eyes on the middle of the river where the Mexican attack was struggling against the steady barrage of aimed rifle fire. The severely decimated Jiménez Regiment had advanced two hundred feet and still had two hundred more when they broke to their right, seeking shelter on the flat, low island. The Matamoros Regiment, no longer sheltered by the Jiménez Regiment surged forward. They were nearly halfway to the Texas side of the Rio Grande. Screaming and waving their bayoneted muskets, they surged forward through the churning water.

Will noticed, as many of Crockett's riflemen were hurriedly reloading, the *soldados* surging through the shallow water approached their side of the river. From the rifle blinds, shots rang out, slapping into the bodies of the tightly packed, surging Mexican infantry. To his right, Will felt the earth shake as all three of Captain Carey's guns loosed a hail of broken iron and bullets into the flank of the Mexican line. A few seconds later, the artillery battery closest to Crockett ripped into the other side of the Mexican line.

A rolling cloud of smoke floated on top the river from the artillery pieces, masking the water and the soldados. Will peered into the smoky gloom, waiting to see the crushing mass of men surging toward the shore. A cold breeze stirred the smoke and as it dissipated, Will saw at least a hundred men streaming back across the river, while several score more were splashing ashore on the island, seeking what shelter as could be found.

The white uniformed men from the San Luis Potosi Battalion, a militia regiment, were shell-shocked as the men ahead of them disappeared in the blasts of a half-dozen cannon. Nearly a score of their own number crumpled into the water, as fragments from the cannon hit them too. Ignoring their officers and NCOs they turned en masse and retreated to their side of the river.

From his left, Will heard a smattering of gunfire from Fannin's location, opposite the narrow island. It sounded like his men were firing on the elements of the Jiménez and Matamoros Regiments that were sheltering on the island. A rattling of musket fire erupted from the island as the *soldados* reacted. A deep-throated roar announced one of Captain Dickinson's cannons raking a section of the narrow island.

The island was little more than a long, narrow sandbar. A few trees survived the frequent floods that covered it when the river ran high. However, from the soil sprang thickets of scrub brush and high grasses that gave the professionals of Santa Anna's army some cover from which they returned fire at Fannin's defensive position. The six guns in Dickinson's two batteries fired one by one, as the gunners sought to target the sniping *soldados*.

Will found Crockett standing between two field guns in Captain Carey's battery closest to the tip of the island and joined him. Crockett peered over the earthen embankment looking at the puffs of smoke denoting where *soldados* had taken shelter and were now firing on Fannin's men.

Will turned and said, "David, why don't you bring some of your riflemen over here. The angle of the embankment won't let us traverse the cannon to face the island, but we can put some riflemen here and do some good." Crockett, with all the speed his forty-nine years could muster, emptied out several blinds and brought a couple of dozen men back with him.

Will edged away from the earthen wall as several riflemen slipped between him and the cannons. Like before, each sharpshooter was supported by two men reloading. The *soldados* had sought the best cover they could find as they traded shots with Fannin's men. Crockett's sharpshooters sent raking fire into the flank of the Mexican *soldados* on the island. Their rate of fire was slow and deliberate. Will watched the nearest marksman take nearly a minute between shots, as he waited for a target to appear.

After a quarter hour of the rattle of musketry and the steady booming of Dickinson's batteries, Will heard cheering from his left flank. He rushed to the side of the battery and looked to the river. He saw a stream of blue jacketed men splashing and swimming back to the Mexican side of the river. A slight swelling along the center of the island shielded the retreating *soldados* from musket and cannon fire from the Texians' fixed positions. However, Will's vantage allowed him to view the river downstream from the ford, where he saw at least a hundred men climb out of the chilly Rio Grande.

He heard Crockett's men joining the rest of the defenders shouting, "Huzzah!" He couldn't keep a large smile from his face as Will realized they had likely crippled two of the three battalions that composed Santa Anna's Vanguard brigade. Crockett slapped him on the back and said, "Buck, you look like a cat that caught the mouse."

Will tried to erase his jubilant grin when he said, "That was very well done, David. Let the other officers know that we'll meet shortly? I want to know the disposition of each unit, included any casualties."

Will was back at the makeshift headquarters to the rear of the battle, when Captain Carey and Jim Bowie arrived from their positions along the ford. Seguin arrived a few minutes later, his horse channeling his rider's enthusiasm as it pranced toward the assembled officers. Crockett and Captain Dickinson came in last. Crockett's face was somber while Dickinson appeared to be near tears. When the two arrived, Crockett said, "I regret to be the bearer of ill news, Colonel Travis, but Colonel Fannin was killed while rallying his command."

The command tent had been pitched in a field that his Excellency had ordered the axe-wielding pioneers to clear. Colonel Juan Almonte watched the last of the officers file into the tent. He had no doubt about how this meeting would go. Almonte knew only too well that his Excellency accepted only victory. As the last to enter, he waved the guards to wait at a nearby campfire and closed the flap.

A long table was situated in the center of the tent. At the head, stood his Excellency, Santa Anna. At forty-two, he was of average height and his Castilian features and dark-brown hair stood in stark contrast to the shorter statured, swarthy Mestizos that composed the substantial majority of not only his army but also the people of the Mexican Republic. His hazel eyes blazed in anger at the men around the table.

To his right, Major Montoya, acting commander of the Permanente Dolores Regiment, stood with his hands clasped behind his back. The young man inherited command of the regiment when the body of General Mora had washed up on the bank of el Rio Bravo del Norte, as Almonte referred to the Rio Grande. As his Excellency tore into the young major, Colonel Almonte couldn't decide if he was more embarrassed for the major or his Excellency's inability to contain himself.

"How could your men fail to reach the opposite bank, Major? These are nothing more than norteamericano pirates! Pirates!" Spittle flew from the dictator's lips as the young officer remained silent. "Bah! Next time, you'll do better or I'll know why."

Almonte silently let out a breath he had not realized he was holding when the young major replied, "Yes, sir, Excellency!"

Almonte saw him turn on Colonel Jose Romero, battalion commander of the Permanente Matamoros Battalion, eyes still blazing in anger, "What the hell happened, Colonel? Your men were behind the Jimenez Battalion and when they broke ranks, they at least tried to force their way to below the ford. Your men, they just broke and ran. Why?"

General Filisola had remained silent until that moment, but as his Excellency's second-in-command, he broke silence, "Excellency! I think that Major Montoya and Colonel Romero reacted as best as they could. Who was to know that these pirates would be able to fortify the Camino Real with artillery along el Bravo del Norte?"

Santa Anna glowered at his second-in-command and snapped at him, "Our intelligence suggested no such thing, General."

Filisola helplessly spread his hands and shrugged, "Then our intelligence was lacking, Excellency."

Almonte watched as Santa Anna threw himself into his camp chair, which creaked alarmingly, and after a heavy sigh, asked, "General, where does today's action leave our Vanguard brigade?"

Filisola took the chair to his Excellency's right and pulled a sheet of paper out, and said, "It could be worse, Excellency. Major Montoya's Lancers have one hundred ninety men effective. We have forty-eight wounded, another twenty-five killed and twenty-seven missing, but presumed dead." He found a second sheet and read, "The Permanente Jimenez Battalion." His lips pursed as he continued, "Of two hundred seventy-four men, one hundred thirty-two are effective. Seventy-one men are wounded, thirty-seven dead and thirty-four are missing, but presumed dead."

The faces of the men sitting around the table were glum as Filisola picked up a third sheet of paper, "The Permanente Matamoros Battalion, "Of two hundred seventy-two men, one hundred eighteen are effective. Eighty-six men are wounded, twenty-eight dead, and another forty are missing and presumed dead." He took the last sheet and read, "From the Activo San Luis Potosi Battalion, of four hundred fifty-two men, four hundred seventeen are effective. Twenty-five were wounded, eight dead, and two missing and presumed dead."

Filisola's face was ashen as he continued, "Excellency, while we have eight artillery pieces that will arrive at some point tonight, the balance of our brigade can currently field eight hundred sixty men or so."

Almonte blanched. There were 230 men wounded in their camp this evening, and in their haste to come north, his Excellency had overlooked most of their medical supplies. He wondered how many would ever serve their country again. Of the two hundred or more who died today, none would be buried in their church's cemetery. He closed his eyes and said a prayer to the Blessed Virgin to watch over all those who would never know a Christian burial.

Chapter 8

The fresh-turned dirt released an earthy scent as frost clung to withered weeds in the chill of the early morning. Will watched a lay chaplain holding a service for two of Juan Seguin's Tejano cavalrymen who died the previous day. The two graves joined a half-dozen crosses which had been planted following the battle that claimed James Fannin's life as well as Santa Anna's hopes of a quick crossing on the 16th.

Thinking back, Will counted his blessings after he had been deployed with the 36th Infantry's 56th Combat Brigade there had been no fatalities, at least until the freak accident which stranded him in the body of William B. Travis. Even when he was on active duty, his unit suffered no fatalities in the battle for Fallujah. But intellectually, he could wrap his mind around the fact that casualties were an integral part of nineteenth century warfare. *"Even so"* he mused, *"I hate losing a single soldier. It is all well and good that men are willing to die for their country and their freedom, but far better that Santa Anna's soldiers are the ones doing the dying."*

Although observing the service from a distance, Will removed his hat as the Catholic layman gave a benediction for the two Tejanos. They died while defending against an attempted crossing by the lancers of the Dolores Cavalry Regiment. Since the battle, two days before, Santa Anna had not sat idly by. While he made no further attempt to ford the river where the Camino Real crossed it, he used his remaining lancers to make forays across the river at several spots both up and downstream from the ford. In these cases, Seguin's mounted Tejanos had spotted the attempts and used their own mobility and firepower to deny the lancers a foothold on the Texas shore. Seguin had reported they killed or wounded a dozen lancers, against the two he lost.

Will knew, sooner rather than later, Santa Anna would receive reinforcements, and when that happened, he mentally conceded that the dictator could force his way across the river, simply by flanking his static line.

That afternoon, this was the topic that brought Colonels Crockett, Bowie, and Grant, as well as Captains Dickinson and Seguin, to meet with Will under the open-air tarp, serving as their headquarters. "Gentlemen," Will said, "Santa Anna's made several attempts to get a foothold on our side of the Rio Grande." He looked toward Seguin, "How long before your men are unable to keep Santa Anna's cavalry on their side of the river?"

Bowie stepped forward and placed his hand on Seguin's shoulder, "Buck, Seguin's men ain't just brave, but they are our best mounted troops! I, for one, have confidence not just in their ability but also in their loyalty."

Will stared nonplused at Bowie, surprised at the knife fighter's passionate appeal. He admired Juan Seguin's fierce determination. Will didn't think that he suffered from the rampant racism that was prevalent in this day and age. He felt a flash of heat as his face turned red. He realized he was getting angry at Bowie, and he struggled to stuff the anger back down as he responded. "Jim, I have every confidence in Juan, Captain Seguin and all of his men. If I wasn't clear about that, I'm sorry. But that's not what I was talking about. None of us should have any illusions that over the next few days Santa Anna's cavalry will receive enough reinforcements that will enable him to put three or four hundred cavalry across the Rio Grande at a place and timing of his choosing. What happens, then, Jim?"

When Bowie slumped back, Will could see the knife fighter's eyes were dark circles. His normally ruddy complexion was pallid. He shrugged and drew a ragged breath, "We can meet them wherever they cross and do to them again what we did to them here." With that, he sank down into a camp chair, exhausted.

Will watched as everyone else tried talking over each other, until Crockett slammed his palm down on the field table, shaking its fragile frame. The men stopped talking and looked at Crockett with shocked expressions. Will shared their surprise, as Crockett had been the model of a frontier gentleman since his arrival. "Now, fellas, I have no doubt that we could knock some more of Santa Anna's teeth out of his head, but at what cost? We have been fortunate to have the wide Rio Grande between us and them. When we lose that, we lose our greatest advantage. Our artillery is entrenched, facing Mexico. If we need to turn and face Santa Anna's army on this side, how many guns can we quickly maneuver around?"

Will was content to let Crockett talk. At nearly fifty years of age, he was nearly twice as old as Will's twenty-seven years, and showed the seasoning of those years. Plus, Will thought, what Crockett had said mirrored his own thoughts. The Tennessean continued, "So happens, been thinking about this since we whipped Santa Anna two days ago. What we need is another ambush."

Will saw the thoughtful expressions on the other men's faces as Crockett explained, "It won't work here on the Rio Grande again. You can look across the river and see Santa Anna's brought his own cannons up here and I bet he's got the solid shot that we ain't got. Now, gentlemen, as I once said during our late troubles with the Indians, I ain't one to retreat, but sometimes you gotta advance to the rear to go forward." The men chuckled over Crockett's well-regarded wit.

"But let's say that we pull our artillery back, maybe as early as tonight, and in their place, we put some Quaker guns and perhaps trick ol' Santa Anna into thinking we're all still sitting pretty here on this side of the Rio Grande, while the balance of our army sets up another ambush on the Nueces."

Will carefully considered Crockett's words and thought he saw the full tactical picture of the proposal, but asked, "David, how do we keep Santa Anna from following hard on our army's heels?"

Nodding thoughtfully, the old frontier fighter replied, "We leave a holding force here. We keep enough men that when Santa Anna comes a'calling we greet him in the manner to which he's become accustomed. We give him a bloody lip and a black eye then we retreat. Our rearguard will stay just far enough ahead of the dictator's army so that he nips at our heels like a bloodhound trying to tree a porcupine. Until he runs right into our bear trap on the Nueces."

Will weighed the proposal and noted that the other men around the camp table were visibly impressed with it. Between Walt Disney and John Wayne, Will knew Crockett had earned a reputation on the frontier with his hunting prowess and Indian fighting skills, but he hadn't realized that Crockett's flair for strategy met or exceeded his own. Bowie stood back up, looking much better to Will's eyes and said, "That's a damn promising idea Crockett. Sign me up to lead the delaying force!"

Colonel Grant added, in his soft Scottish accent, "You'll be taking upon yourself one of the hardest things to pull off in war, Jim. Any retreat can be hell, but a fighting retreat is, I think, the most difficult. Every engagement with the Mexican forces runs you the risk of being cut off and destroyed, but do too little and you may risk breaking contact with Santa Anna's force and letting them choose an alternate route."

Crockett and the other officers expressed their agreement at what Will thought was sage advice from the Scotsman. Will decided it was time for him to weigh in, "David, your idea is a capital one. Will you work with Jim to make it happen? I think the two of you can make a go of it. Take Seguin's cavalry, you'll need the best scouts and mounted fighters that we have. That will leave me, Colonel Grant, and our artillery captains to set a warm welcome for Santa Anna at the Nueces."

Will stamped his feet and swung his arms, trying to keep warm. Dawn was more than an hour away and the temperature hovered near freezing, as he watched his breath in the frosty morning air. He blew a heavy sigh of relief when the last cannon rolled down the road, heading north. He had been awake for most of the night, as Carey and Dickinson had quietly replaced their field pieces in their emplaced batteries with black painted logs. In the predawn, Will couldn't tell much of a difference when looking at the batteries, but wondered how the emplacements would look from less than two hundred away. He feared that anyone with a spyglass would see through the subterfuge. He shook his head and tried to push any doubt from his mind. He reminded himself, they had rolled the die and fretting over it wasn't productive.

As Crockett had ineloquently said, there were more volunteers to stay and fight on the river than he could shake a stick at. In addition to Seguin's cavalry, which now numbered forty men, Crockett and Bowie had selected another fifty men to stay. There were not enough mounts to allow for more. Will fervently prayed it was enough to bait the trap.

While the artillery and Ward's Battalion were already marching northward to the Nueces, the remainder of the men stayed behind for the day. Will's rationale was simple. If the trick with the Quaker guns failed, and Santa Anna attempted anything today, he was confident that with nearly five hundred men, he could stop the Mexicans or at least make the cost so high it would delay Santa Anna.

As evening came and the sun was setting low, Will knew it was time to pull back all his men but the volunteers selected to remain. As he prepared to give the order to march, Will saw Crockett approaching, concern carved into his face. "Buck, we have a problem," he said quietly, as he gently took Will by the elbow and moved away to where they could speak privately. "While we were down at the river working on better blinds for our riflemen, Jim collapsed. I've seen a preacher caught in a whorehouse looking better than him."

The two returned to the river where Will found Bowie lying on a blanket, behind one of the blinds. His face was pasty white. When he put his hand to Bowie's forehead, Will found the knife fighter burning with fever. Bowie cracked his eyes open as Will knelt over him and struggled to sit up, "It ain't nothing I can't shake off, Buck. You go on and get out of here."

Bowie's voice lacked the strength his tone tried to convey. Crockett knelt across from Will and placed his hand on Bowie's forehead. "Tarnation, Jim. I could cook me up a mess of grits and bacon on your head."

Bowie growled at Will and Crockett and attempted to toss his head, trying to remove the hand, "Don't be giving me any of your homespun wit, David. I need to be here with my boys. And you know it!"

Crockett removed his hand and in a voice that only the three of them could hear, "Are you willing to bet not just your life but the lives of all these men that you'll be better tomorrow, Jim?"

Bowie collapsed back onto the blanket, his breathing ragged and his face gray from the exertion of talking, "Damn you to Hell, Crockett. Bet it makes you feel all good inside to be right so damned often." Will watched the interplay between the frontiersman and the knife fighter. He was learning to appreciate Crockett was happy to give the rank and file soldiers the impression he was just a 'high private' as the Tennessean phrased it, but the truth was, he had no problem influencing the men around him, from the lowest private up to the highest-ranking officer. It was amazing to behold, and reminded Will it was that charisma and skill with people which previously earned Crockett three terms in the US Congress.

Will heard the ticking of his timepiece in his vest pocket as silence descended on the three men. Finally, Crockett turned to him and asked, "Well, Buck, what's the plan, now?"

Exhaling sharply, Will replied, "Grant, Cary, and Dickinson can set the ambush without me. Let's see if we can get you loaded into a wagon, Jim." Bowie didn't respond. He lay there with his eyes closed, each breath rattling in his throat.

Will looked up and saw the clouds obscuring the moon. The remainder of the army slipped away a company at a time until all that remained were the ninety volunteers. He stood within the entrenchment where the battery closest to the ford was placed, next to Crockett and Seguin. They peered across the Rio Grande, the other shore masked by the heavy cloud cover. Although they couldn't see them, they could hear men digging entrenchment positions for Santa Anna's artillery. His stomach cramped a bit as Will realized that the revolution was dependent on what he, Crockett, and Seguin could accomplish. There were more butterflies fluttering than the ones in his stomach, as the thought came to him that he had no idea what Santa Anna would do next.

Chapter 9

A small stove radiated enough heat in the corner of the large, spacious tent, that Colonel Juan Almonte moved his camp chair further away from it. As aide-de-camp to his Excellency, Almonte took notes of the meeting. Santa Anna paced back and forth in front of the table, around which several regimental and brigade commanders sat. Almonte inwardly cringed as his Excellency verbally eviscerated the Vanguard Brigade's commander, Juaquin Sesma. "Juaquin, it has been three days since those pirates kept your men from the north bank of the Rio Bravo del Norte. Why the hell aren't your men on the other side of the river?"

General Sesma wore a pained expression as he tried to explain the failing, "Excellency, we have made several forays across the Rio Bravo, but these pirates and their traitorous Mexican allies have contested every attempt, costing us lives each time."

The longer they were on this, the wrong side of the river the more His Excellency's temper was fraying, and General Sesma had taken the brunt of that temper over the past few days. Almonte heard this all before, from the reports he collected. It was nothing new. But Sesma's mention of the Tejanos caused Santa Anna to explode anew. "I'll personally cut off the *cojones* of Zavala when I capture him and shove them down his throat!" Almonte regretted Lorenzo de Zavala's betrayal against Santa Anna, when his Excellency had been forced by the instability in Central Mexico to set aside the constitution and rule as dictator. He knew the betrayal galled Santa Anna ever since word reached Mexico City that Zavala was working with the *norteamericano* pirates, Stephen Austin and Sam Houston to rip Texas away from Mexico.

When his Excellency was this angry, Almonte loathed putting himself into the crosshairs, but he sighed, acknowledging his duty to Santa Anna. "Excellency, in the unlikely event that General Sesma's lancers are unable to turn the rebel's flank, the latest reports from General Gaona show he will arrive within the next couple of days. I'm certain he's force-marching his men here, as you instructed. Time is on our side. Once Gaona's brigade arrives, we'll have two thousand five hundred men at your disposal to force a crossing."

"Juan, time is not on our side!" His Excellency shot back, slamming his fist on the table, causing an unsecured map to slide off, landing face down on the ground. "God knows what those pirates are doing on the other side of the river as we sit and do nothing!" He glared at the brigade commander, "Either find a way across the river, or I'll find someone who will!"

Almonte leaned over, rescuing the map from where it fell and as he set it back on the table, he noticed it was the region between the Rio Bravo and the Nueces. Despite himself, he could only wonder if their army would ever reach San Antonio de Bexar.

Two days had passed since Will saw the balance of his little army marching northward, toward the Nueces River. The day before, the eight artillery pieces on the Mexican side of the river fired a few rounds of solid shot into the earthen embankments behind which they sheltered. He knew it was a matter of time before Santa Anna sent his infantry storming across the river. He amended his thought, "Assuming, of course, that we can keep his lancers from flanking us."

Will sat atop his horse, next to Captain Seguin and watched a few of the Captain's men come splashing from the river where they had placed a trap. Since the previous morning the lancers had patrolled up and down the river, obviously looking for likely spots to exploit. That's what brought Will and Seguin, along with a majority of the Tejano cavalry to this likely locale, where a wide sandbar was submerged across most of the width of the Rio Grande. Will turned, and asked, "Juan, do you think they'll try crossing here?"

The Tejano shrugged, "It's a more likely spot than most, Colonel. I sure hope so, otherwise we've wasted our time running those ropes between the stakes." Their hiding place behind a copse of mesquite trees and dense scrub brush afforded them a view of the river at the likely crossing.

As if on cue, through the thorny branches, Will saw a company of lancers riding alongside the opposite side of the river. With the river rippling over it, the sandbank was easy to see from the southern shore, and a couple of men, in their blue and red jackets guided their horses into the shallow and fast flowing water. When they reached the midpoint, the two men wheeled around and waved to their waiting compatriots. Will saw a resplendently dressed officer, wearing a deep-blue officer's coat, leading the column into the river. In place of the steel helmets worn by the lancers, the officer wore a bicorn hat with a green, white, and red cockade fixed to the front. Will stifled a laugh when Seguin leaned over and whispered, "Santa Anna's sending over his peacocks now."

No sooner had the gaudily dressed officer's horse came to the end of the sandbank, starting into deeper water than the animal became entangled in the rope ensnared stakes running parallel to the shoreline. Several lancers leapt forward on their mounts to help the officer when they found their own horses fouled in the ropes, snaking below the surface of the murky water. Will smiled grimly as a horse twisted and crashed into another entangled horse, spilling both riders into the chilly water.

He nodded to Seguin, "Your command, Captain." Seguin flashed an elated grin and pulled a shotgun from a scabbard on his saddle and shouted in Spanish, "Up and at them, boys!" The Tejano captain dug his heels into his horse's flanks and charged onto the bank of the river, followed by two dozen men. Seguin hammered back his shotgun and pointed it in the direction of the peacock, pulling the trigger. The gun kicked in his hand as the dandy jerked in the saddle. As the rest of Seguin's mounted men rode along the shoreline they emptied shotguns and pistols into the milling and disorganized mass of lancers, churning the water, turning red where lancers fell.

Will remained back, observing the short firefight. His right hand ran along the woodgrain on the butt of his shotgun, which remained in its scabbard. Seguin and his men were holding the lancers at bay. Will guessed the lancers had attempted to cross in company strength, perhaps forty men. Several horses remained entangled in the ropes, as other riderless horses trotted along the shoreline. The remnants of the lancers fled back to their side of the wide river, leaving several bodies bobbing in the water, including the one Seguin referred to as a peacock. From Will's vantage point, it appeared that half of the lancers returned to the southern shoreline as Seguin's troopers wheeled around and rode north. Will galloped over beside Seguin, slapping him on the back, "Well done, Juan!" Yet again, Santa Anna had been denied the Texas bank of the Rio Grande.

Colonel Almonte stood outside his Excellency's headquarters tent, watching the troop of lancers return from the latest attempt to cross el Rio Bravo del Norte. Forty men rode out, led by General Sesma. Only a score of men returned. Almonte craned his neck looking for Sesma, but no matter where he looked, he saw neither the general nor his fine stallion. A lancer, with sergeant chevrons, spotted Almonte and guided his horse to the Colonel. "Sir, it was a trap. We found a spot a couple of leagues down river and it looked promising for both our infantry and artillery, but when we tried crossing, the pirates had staked the river with crisscrossing strands of rope, tripping up our horses." Almonte could see where this was headed, but he bade the sergeant to continue.

"When most of our men were entangled in the trap, the traitors attacked. General Sesma was the first to fall."

When Almonte informed his Excellency of Sesma's failure, Santa Anna turned to Almonte, "At least he had the decency to atone for his failure, Juan. That leaves me without a commander for the Vanguard Brigade." Almonte watched his Excellency stride over to the table centered in the middle of the tent, where he snatched up a sheet of paper. Inking a quill, he scratched on the paper for a moment then held it up, and exclaimed, "Juan, you shall command the Vanguard Brigade now. General Almonte!"

With a forced smile on his face, Almonte accepted the promotion from his Excellency. He gave a crisp salute and replied, "Thank you, Excellency. With your permission, I shall go and check on the men." Waved away by Santa Anna, Almonte exited the tent with a sinking feeling and went to find the three regimental commanders, certain that this was not the way he wanted to rise to the rank of general. The cold breeze from the north, blowing an ill wind.

The northerly breeze lacked the chill from the morning, as Will stood behind the artillery entrenchment, next to one of the blackened tree trucks which had fooled the Mexican army for several days. He shook his head, wondering if the officers staring across the river saw only what they wanted to see. He couldn't imagine how the masquerade had continued for four days. He hoped if the roles were reversed he wouldn't be hoodwinked by something like the Quaker guns sticking out of the earthen embankments. The dust cloud to the south, made by the marching feet of another brigade, indicated even if the trickery was maintained, Santa

Anna would force a crossing at some point along the river very shortly.

That night, Crockett's riflemen sheltered behind the artillery embankments. The occasional cannon shot echoed across the river as the round thudded harmlessly into the earthen walls protecting the riflemen's positions. A few hundred feet back, Will sat next to a small campfire with Crockett and Seguin, discussing their options. "Buck, I have to say that this has worked far better than I would have expected. I figured that old Santa Anna would come at us quick as lightning, but instead, he's been at us like a herd of turtles."

Will chortled at Crockett's comment, "True, David, but I suspect he's about to give it another go tomorrow. How much damage do you think we're going to inflict when they come knocking?"

Crockett scratched at the graying stubble on his chin and replied, "Well, Buck, I'm not exactly inclined to stay here long enough to shake ol' Santa Anna's hand when he comes prancing across the Rio Grande, but yeah, I think we can make it look like he's been wrastlin' with a polecat. Biggest problem is that most of our rifles went north with Grant. If we have forty rifles betwixt all of us here I'd be surprised."

Will grimaced. He had counted the number of rifles and his tally matched the Tennessean's. In his downtime, he thought back over his own training as a rifleman in the 144th Infantry. The camaraderie of the fire team was the glue holding an infantry company together, as far as he was concerned. That same cohesion didn't exist here, but he had a thought, "David, what would you think about trying the same tactic we used before. What if we created ten teams of four men each? The best, like before, is the shooter, while the other three men load like hell. When the Mexicans get within a hundred feet, we get out of here."

Crockett nodded, "Might could work, Buck. But if they send cavalry across we need to skedaddle when they get halfway. If it's infantry, then a hundred feet might work. But we'd be in the range of their muskets if they get off a volley."

Juan Seguin listened to Will and Crockett up to that point. He interjected, "With your permission, Colonel Travis, I'd like to send half my men north along the Camino Real and find a spot a few miles ahead to set up our next ambush. I know of a lovely arroyo that would make for a delightful surprise for *el Presidente's* men."

The 23rd of February dawned cold, the sun retreating behind heavy cloud cover, as light rain mixed with snow flurries whisking across the surface of the Rio Grande. The top of the earthen embankment was slick with a thin glaze of ice. Will knelt by Crockett and two other men behind the earthen embankment and realized that in a world gone forever, today would be the start of Santa Anna's siege of the Alamo. His lips curled into a tight smile as he wondered what changes would bloom from the flower planted by avoiding entrapment at the Alamo.

Across the river, Santa Anna revealed his plan when Will saw the regimental standard of the Permanente Aldama Regiment come bobbing into view as the men under its banner filtered through the mesquite trees to either side of the Camino Real on the Mexican side of the river. Another banner flew behind the men assembling on the shoreline. The *soldados* of the Activo Toluca battalion were assembling behind the veterans from Aldama. A single clarion note pealed melodically across the Rio Grande as the four hundred men of the battalion stepped into the shallow, swift-flowing water. The officers and NCOs moved along the battalion front, trying to keep the men moving forward across the ford.

The *soldados* of the Aldama Regiment had taken barely a dozen steps before Will heard the flint on Crockett's rifle strike the pan, igniting the charge at the base of the barrel, sending the lead ball flying at the Mexican line at nine hundred feet per second. A quick glance over the icy, earthen barrier saw an officer topple from his horse. Nine more shots exploded from the hidden Texian riflemen.

Crockett snatched the rifle from Will's hands, replacing it with an empty one. The older man threw the rifle to his shoulder, where he paused to line up the sights. A couple of seconds passed, and he fired again. Will tore his eyes away from the southern shore and hurried to reload the gun that Crockett had traded him.

Despite the frigid water, the Aldama and Toluca battalions moved as swiftly as the current allowed, covering half the distance in a little less than three minutes. In that time, Crockett's riflemen fired more than three hundred rounds into the packed ranks of Mexican infantry. Will noticed that two hundred feet separated his small command from the advancing men. As he traded rifles with Crockett he shouted over the din, "A couple more rounds, David, and we need to get out of here."

The men of the Aldama battalion sensing victory, rushed through the waist-high water, muskets raised high, keeping their powder dry. When they were still more than a hundred feet away, Will tapped Crockett on the shoulder and said, "Time's about up, David. Let's get back to Seguin and the horses!"

Crockett lowered his rifle, acrid smoke curling out of the dirty barrel, and turned and started jogging toward the line of horses. A shout to the other men and they were sprinting toward their horses, too. When the Mexican line saw the retreating Texians running away, an enraged shout echoed across the water. Their prey was escaping. Their discipline broke and enraged men brought their muskets down from over their heads and in ones and twos fired at the backs of the retreating Texians.

Will was one of the last men running toward their horses and felt a buzzing sound zip by his ear and heard a wet, smacking sound to his right. He saw a spray of red explode from the back of the rifleman running beside him, and saw the man crumple to the ground. Under his breath, Will swore as he saw the large hole the .69 caliber ball made in the back of his fellow soldier.

As he reached the horses most of the riflemen were already riding north. Juan Seguin sat astride his mount , holding Will's reins. As he grabbed them from the Tejano, he chanced another glance toward the riverbank, more than a hundred yards away, and saw the bodies of four of his men splayed on the ground, dead. The flag of the Aldama battalion waved atop one of the gun emplacements. Hundreds of *soldados* swarmed over the emplacements, running in their direction. Will wheeled around and followed Seguin as they urged their horses to a gallop.

Chapter 10

Will clung to the galloping horse, keeping his eyes fixed to the small of Seguin's back. He was grateful for Travis' muscle memories. If he had to rely on his own twenty-first century ability to sit on a horse, he'd likely be a ventilated pin cushion for Santa Anna's *soldados*. For what seemed like the hundredth time, Will wondered if he would wake up and find all this was but a dream. It was too fantastic to be real. Yet he found himself riding a horse, hell-bent for leather, behind Juan Seguin on the Camino Real. He chanced a look behind and saw the road meandering toward the distant river. There was no sign of pursuit, yet.

If this were nothing more than simple random chance, Will wondered, *"What the hell am I doing here? I could take all the knowledge of the next fifty years and make a fortune that would make Rockefeller look like a pauper."*

Gripping the reins tighter and pulling his elbows in, he urged his horse to stay up with the accomplished Tejano horseman ahead of him. He continued reasoning, *"This is too great a coincidence to simply be random fate.*" Since joining the army after 9/11, life had pulled him away from the faith of his youth, but he'd never doubted there was something greater out there in the universe. He chuckled as he galloped along, and thought, "To be at this time and place in history makes a rather compelling argument for divine intervention."

He followed the thought down the mental rabbit hole, "There's no reason that God would dump me in Travis' body if he intended me to die at the Alamo. Not likely to happen that way, now."

He scanned the ground ahead of Seguin and wondered how much further they had to ride before reaching the arroyo. "We'll get there soon enough." Will thought, then followed his mind back to the Gordian knot on which he was mentally working. Thinking about the world he knew, he couldn't help but dwell on how screwed up it had become. Dictators like Hitler, Stalin, and Mao had killed hundreds of millions of people over the last century. Will's mind rebounded against the thought that perhaps he was supposed to stop all that.

In the distance, he saw several riders urging their horses over the shallow embankment of a dry creek bed. The arroyo was less than half mile away. As he attempted to turn his focus back to the present, another thought came unbidden to him. "Be the very best William Barret Travis that you can be. Don't be so pretentious as to think that God put you here to change the whole world."

As his horse navigated up a wagon trail that cut across the arroyo, he decided on two things. Do the right thing as Travis, and survive the next week.

Several men stood well back from the arroyo, collecting the reins from others, who handed their mounts to the handlers and headed back to the arroyo with their weapons. Will walked back to the arroyo and found Seguin making a few corrections to where some of his men were positioned. Will joined him as Crockett also walked up, rubbing his backside, saying, "Tarnation, I ain't as young as I once was, and riding pell-mell don't sit near as well as it used to."

Seguin smiled slyly at the Tennessean and said, "Colonel Crockett, I was riding behind you, and I can assure you, you didn't sit very well on that horse anyway."

Crockett smiled ruefully, "I guess I had that coming. No one told me you could use that tongue of yours prettier than a five-dollar whore."

As Seguin sputtered, Crockett turned away and directed his riflemen to places along the top of the arroyo, providing a good field of fire. The conversation forgotten, Will noticed that Crockett was setting up his riflemen to catch any advance from the south in a deadly crossfire.

He commented on it, "Good placement, David. Let's hope they decide to stick their neck in this noose. How well do you think we did back on the river?"

Crockett said, "I think we likely took out the better part of a hundred men back on the Rio Grande. And we lost four in the retreat. I think it likely that Santa Anna's boys ain't going to be too far behind us. He led out with his Infantry, but give him a bit of time and he'll have his cavalry out in front."

Will walked behind their line, along the arroyo and saw that Seguin's Tejanos, with their shotguns and pistols were closely spread on either side of the road, playing to the advantage of their short range. Crockett's riflemen were spread out further along the exterior flanks. Given their limited numbers, it seemed a solid plan to Will. He found Crockett between one of his riflemen and one of the Tejanos, a short distance to the left of the road. Will's boots crunched on the rocky ground as he knelt by Crockett, who squatted behind a stunted mesquite tree. His rifle lay balanced where a branch extended from the gnarled trunk.

After he found a bit of scrub brush directly to Crockett's left, Will checked the load in his shotgun, making sure the primer pan was closed. Satisfied his weapon was ready, he looked up and saw the gray, overcast day was giving way to an even darker twilight when in the distance he spied a detachment of Mexican cavalry. The lancers, in their blue and red jackets, looked cold and miserable as they wound their way down the narrow road, approaching the arroyo.

The Camino Real carved a long, steep path through the arroyo, where wagon tracks had long ago eaten away at the creek bed. Dense brush and mesquite trees choked the banks on both sides of the road. As the lancers neared, it was evident Santa Anna was taking no chances. The narrow wagon tracks were packed with a long column of cavalry. It appeared the remaining lancers of the Dolores Cavalry Regiment were approaching his line. He leaned over to Crockett, and quietly said, "Whenever you think best, David."

He watched Crockett as the frontiersman allowed the leading horsemen to enter the dry bed of the arroyo. Crockett fired his rifle, tumbling the nearest lancer from the saddle. The Tejanos, closest to the lancers, fired their shotguns, muskets and pistols into the densely packed lancers. At ranges as low as twenty feet, the Tejano's volley devastated the lancers in the lead. Will watched dozens of men toppled from their saddles, many of whom were crushed beneath their panicked horses. Crockett's riflemen added their confusion as the Texians' aimed fire focused on the splendidly attired officers.

More quickly than he liked, Will saw the lancers' NCOs react to the ambush, restoring order and pushing their fellow men at the defenders. Most of the lancers were forced to dismount to move beyond the carnage centered where the road bisected the arroyo. As Will started to reload, Crockett reached over and grabbed his arm, "No time for that now, Buck. They'll be on us in two shakes of a coon's tail." Crockett drew a hunting knife from his belt. Will stood and drew the cavalry sword, hanging from his belt, and joined the determined frontiersman.

In bed of the arroyo below, Will saw several dismounted lancers making their way along the bottom of the steep banks, the one in the lead still holding his lance before him. The lead lancer spotted Will and Crockett and lunged forward, thrusting the razor-sharp point at Will's abdomen. He twisted his body away, and dodged as the lance's point skewered the air where he had just been. He felt his heart pounding in his chest, adrenaline surging through his body as he leapt down from the arroyo's lip and crashed into the surprised lancer, who dropped his lance as he tumbled backward into the man behind him.

Will looked down and it registered in his mind he was still holding the sword. He gripped the hilt with both hands and swung it in a wide arc at the panicked lancer. His arms reverberated with a jarring crash as the sword caught the lancer along the collar bone. It took all Will's strength to hold onto the sword, as his opponent slid to the ground, blood pulsing from the gash. Will tumbled to the ground as he struggled to free the blade from where it had wedged into the dying soldier's collarbone.

Sitting on the stones, made smooth by an untold number of flash floods running through the arroyo, the hair on his neck stood on end, as warning bells in his head went off. Will rolled to the left, leaving the sword lodged in the dying lancer. The sound of flint striking a firing pan alerted him to a pistol discharging a few feet in front of him, briefly illuminating the bloody ground. As he landed on his left side, he felt his right arm erupt in pain. He gripped his arm and saw the dying man's companion standing a few paces away. The lancer wore an enraged expression as he dropped the smoking pistol and pulled a wicked looking knife from his belt.

Casting a furtive glance around, Will saw a holstered pistol on the dying lancer to his right. He lunged for it, ignoring the burning pain in his right arm, as the knife cleared the other lancer's sheath. The Mexican lunged toward him with the blade, attempting to stab him. Will yanked the hammer back on the pistol, prayed it was loaded, and pulled the trigger. The sharp edge of the flint slammed down and sparks and smoke splayed from the pan. The pistol discharged in Will's left hand. With less than twelve inches between himself and Will, the lunging Mexican lancer grunted in surprise as the bullet caught him in the chest. His eyes grew wide in shock as he sank to his knees and rolled over, still and lifeless.

The third and last of the nearby lancers let fall a smoking pistol and leaned down and picked up a lance laying at his feet. Despite the deepening twilight, Will saw the hatred stamped on the other man's face as he pointed the heavy, wooden lance at Will's chest. His sword was lodged tight in the first man, and the pistol was empty. Will edged away from the approaching lancer, until he found himself trapped by the crumbling dirt wall of the arroyo. He looked at the lancer, who sneered at him with murder blazing from charcoal eyes. The lancer braced his feet, preparing to lunge, when a hand grabbed at his throat from behind and a blade slashed his windpipe. As blood bubbled through the widening gash, the lancer's eyes lost their fiery focus as he sunk to his knees. Crockett stood behind the collapsing soldier, a grimace of disgust stamped on his face, as he guided the body to the ground.

Shuddering with relief, Will struggled to his feet, taking the hand Crockett extended. He flinched as the pain in his right arm, which felt like a nail being driven by a hammer, threatened to overwhelm him with waves of nausea. He pulled his hand away and saw the dark stain of blood smeared on his fingertips. Crockett noticed and grabbed his arm, not as gently as he might, and ran his own fingers along the wound. "You have the luck of the third time, boy. It's just a graze. An inch to the left and we'd be lucky to save your arm."

After working the sword loose and retrieving it, Will joined Crockett and climbed back to the top of the arroyo. They watched Seguin's men giving way along the center of their line, as the lancers, now on foot, crested the arroyo's slope. With Will's arm still stinging, he felt himself being propelled along by Crockett as they collected the other riflemen on their side of the road. "Boys, get those rifles reloaded." Crockett growled to the men now assembling around him them. They reloaded as quickly as their tired fingers would allow, as the Tejanos along the center of their line began running to their horses, away from the advancing, dismounted lancers.

Will, Crockett, and the dozen men around them, stood oblique to the road, amid the mesquite trees and scrub brush. As the last of the Tejanos ran, toward their mounts, Will watched the surging mass of Mexican lancers, running on foot after the Tejanos, brandishing knives, swords, and lances. While Crockett was the first to reload, the other dozen men finished seconds later. His right arm, numb with pain, Will raised his sword in his left hand and brought it down with a flash, yelling, "Fire!"

A dozen rifles fired in unison toward the charging lancers along the road. At less than fifty feet, every bullet found a target, slamming into the flank of the charging men, dropping more lancers. Stunned by the point-blank rifle fire, the lancers stumbled to a stop, many of them taking cover, ducking behind the bodies of their downed companions. With the brief respite, Will turned to Crockett, "Time to hightail it?"

Crockett nodded, "These lancers got their blood up and they got numbers on us, let's get!"

Twilight was fading fast and night was almost fully upon them, as Will took the reins from a handler and mounted up. His mouth twisted into a frown as his arm twinged in pain. He found Seguin riding at a fast clip at the head of his Tejanos. Each step Will's horse took sent jolts of pain up his arm as he came up beside the Tejano captain. He tried his best to not let the pain show as he said, "Juan, your men did an excellent job back there. If you know of another place down the road where we can teach Santa Anna another lesson, lead on!"

Seguin looked back at his men riding behind him, his face radiating pride. He urged them to a faster clip as they cantered down the road. Will looked behind, but it was too dark to see. He wondered how many empty saddles he would find when they stopped again that night.

General Almonte glimpsed into the night sky and wished the heavy clouds would blow away. He stood on the north bank of el Rio Bravo del Norte and recalled how much he enjoyed gazing into moon-filled nights. He felt scant joy now, and knew the cold and cloudy night was not the reason. An hour earlier, he heard the rattling sound of musket fire from the north. Now, as commander of the Vanguard brigade, whatever transpired would fall on his shoulders. He would know soon enough.

He turned away from the river, walking past the earthen embankments that the Texians had thrown up, he was perplexed at the blackened tree trunks that the enemy had used to fool them. He worried about how long had their artillery been gone, and worse, where it was now?

That thought slipped from his mind as he heard shouts in the distance along with the sound of cavalry arriving in camp. He resisted the urge to run, despite the overwhelming need to learn of what transpired. But as the brigadier of the Vanguard brigade, he reminded himself that it was beneath his dignity to be seen running along like an enlisted man. The lancers of the Dolores Cavalry Regiment had dismounted near his Excellency's headquarters tent, now transferred to the northern side of the river. He arrived just in time to see a disheveled sergeant standing at attention in front of Santa Anna. Almonte knew something was dreadfully wrong. He saw no officers amid the lancers. Was the sergeant the highest-ranking soldier to return?

Almonte walked up and stood next to his Excellency and heard the sergeant responding to an inquiry, "Yes, my President. We were scouting ahead, and where the road crosses an arroyo, we ran into a company of the rebels. They were hidden in the mesquite trees and scrub brush along the north side of the arroyo. Their volley killed or wounded all our officers. We couldn't force our way through the arroyo on horseback, so we dismounted and forced them away from their position." The sergeant paused for a moment, unsure how to continue.

The newly minted general felt his heart sinking as Santa Anna's voice fell into a dangerous pitch, only loud enough for the three of them alone to hear. "And how many of the pirates did you kill?"

With a slight sigh of relief, the sergeant responded, "We killed twelve and captured two more, but their injuries are severe." Almonte's left hand was in his pocket, fingering a rosary, thankful that his Excellency didn't ask about their own casualties.

As Santa Anna returned to his headquarters tent, Almonte guided the sergeant away and when he felt they were far enough away, stopped and asked, "And ours? How many of our lancers did the rebels kill or injure?"

Morosely, the sergeant replied, "Twenty-three of our men were killed, and Forty-five were wounded." Almonte blanched at the news. This was horrible. "How many effective lancers can the Dolores Cavalry Regiment field?"

The sergeant grimaced in response, as he said, "Seventy-five, my General."

A half-dozen miles away from Almonte, as the temperature fell through the evening, Will took counsel with Crockett and Seguin. Each of them pulled their coats closer in, trying to keep the worst of the cold at bay. He asked, "How bad are things, David?"

Crockett replied, "We're down to forty riflemen, Buck. I lost six more men back at the arroyo. Juan has his own report."

Seguin's normally jovial voice was solemn, "Si, Colonel. We're down to thirty-four men in my company. We took a beating from the lancers this evening."

Will sighed. It was worse than he had expected. "That puts us down about twenty percent since dawn. If this cloud of ours has a silver lining it is that we likely inflicted more casualties on Santa Anna's army than we have men here." He paused, running his left hand along the bandage wrapped around his right arm, before he continued, "Whatever may happen tomorrow, I want both of you to know your boys fought exceptionally well today. Y'all should be proud of your men."

Seguin's normally cheerful countenance returned, as he listened to Will's praise.

Crockett gestured toward the men, unrolling bedrolls or rubbing down their tired horses and said, "Much obliged, Buck, but it's those boys that did the fighting and dying today. Don't matter if they're from Bexar, Nashville, or Belfast, they fought like lions. When this war is over, that's the kind of courage that we should write about in our history books. Not the kind that sits over on the Brazos, giving speeches." Will tried to hide a smile as he wondered if he and Seguin might be the first to hear a Crockett campaign speech.

The three men grew quiet, each alone with his thoughts. Will's mind replayed the quick and brutal firefight along the arroyo and as he considered the battle, he realized it was the same regiment that Seguin's men had fought a few days prior as well as the same with which Santa Anna opened the battle on the first day. "You know, David, I haven't seen any other Mexican cavalry other than these lancers with their blue and red jackets." He turned toward Seguin and continued, "What about you, Juan, you see any others?"

Seguin shook his head. "No, just the regiment from Dolores. I doubt those lancers have a hundred men left. *El Presidente* has used them up over the past week. You know, Buck," Seguin said, using Travis' nickname for the first time, "We should stay close by tomorrow morning and see what Santa Anna does. If he sends his lancers in the lead, then we should finish them off. If he sends his *cazadores* forward, then we should probably pull back and draw them north."

Crockett interjected, "*Cazadores*? What in the blazes are those?"

Seguin replied, "Loosely translated, it means hunters. They are the Mexican army's light infantry. They are like the Hessian Jäger units during your own, or I mean, the American Revolution. But they are capable scouts and worse for us, many of them are armed with rifles."

The next morning, the 24th of February brought a light snow flurry to the desert southwest, coating mesquites and prickly pear cactuses with a dusting of white. From the south, instead of the lancers from the Dolores Regiment, Will saw in the distance, moving slowly, blue-uniformed infantry, in skirmish formation. "So much for taking out their cavalry today." Will thought wistfully. With that thought, he ordered his men to start moving north, toward the Nueces.

Chapter 11

The ant crawled from the tree bark onto Will's exposed hand. He squashed the insect and removed his hand from the tree as he spotted a trail of ants along the trunk. He turned to Crockett, who knelt beside him. "How far out do you make them, David?"

Crockett peered through Will's spyglass before replying, "Maybe six, seven hundred yards away."

His breath condensed in the morning chill, but Will thought it a bit warmer than the last few days. To Will, the *cazadores* that moved slowly along and next to the Camino Real were no bigger than the ants crawling along the mesquite tree, but he had become very familiar with the blue-jacketed foes over the last few days. Following the near destruction of the Dolores Cavalry Regiment, Santa Anna had used his light infantry effectively to screen his army. Unfortunately, Will amended.

Since the battle at the arroyo, Will's men had set several ambushes along the road, leaving another dozen of their own dead in their wake. For their trouble, they inflicted forty casualties on Santa Anna's army. The high point of the retreat was watching Crockett shoot an infantry officer from more than four hundred yards away. While Will was frustrated with Santa Anna's newfound wariness of ambushes, he reminded himself, "We slowed him down to scarcely more than a dozen miles a day, and gave Grant and the others plenty of time to set up one hell of a defense on the Nueces River."

Since the previous afternoon, Will had been in contact with the main army. Now, less than a half mile separated him from Colonel Grant. And less than half a mile separated the advancing Mexican *cazadores* from Will, Crockett, and thirty riflemen, who were hidden amid a field of mesquite trees and scrub brush, running alongside the Camino Real. Additionally, Seguin's remaining cavalry, now only twenty-five strong, hid behind a large copse of mesquite trees behind Crockett's riflemen. Will's plan was simple. Crockett and his riflemen would open fire on the advancing *cazadores* at 250 yards. Seguin's men were situated to provide protection to the riflemen when they pulled back toward the main defensive position along the Nueces.

The long minutes ticked by and Will checked his pocket watch a couple of times as the *cazadores* snaked their way closer, along the Camino Real. Although his pocket watch showed only fifteen minutes had elapsed, it felt like an hour had come and gone before Crockett said, "Right about there." He aimed his rifle and fired. Will watched the gray, acrid smoke swirl out of the barrel, then looked downrange where he saw a *soldado* clutch at his arm, as he spun around, falling to the ground. Along the line of riflemen, sheltered amid the scrub brush, another thirty rounds sped toward the

Mexican skirmishers.

As his riflemen hastily reloaded, Will kept his eyes on the *cazadores*, many of whom began running in the direction of Crockett's riflemen. The smoky haze of gunpowder hung in the air, as Crockett's riflemen sent more shots into the advancing skirmish line. He watched the Mexican skirmishers running, and briefly wondered what it would take to manufacture cordite powder. At somewhat less than two hundred yards away, the *cazadores* stopped and returned fire at the sheltered Texian riflemen.

Will instinctively ducked behind the fallen mesquite trunk as a bullet slammed into it less than a foot away from his face. *"Damn,"* Will thought, as he brushed splinters from his jacket, "They've got Baker's rifles!"

Will watched Crockett calmly reload his rifle, sheltering low behind a mesquite tree. When he had reloaded, he exposed only the smallest part needed to aim at a target, fire, and shelter behind the tree, reloading again. A couple of bullets smacked harmlessly into the trunk, inches away from where he had been only an instant before. Will peered through the heavy smoke hugging the ground in front of the riflemen and gauged that all his men were still in the fight. The rifle-armed *cazadores* returned fire, sheltered by the same scrub brush and mesquite trees affording Will's men the same protection.

Beyond the Mexican skirmish line, Will saw a battalion of white-jacketed infantry deploying to the left of the Camino Real. The normally crisp lines were broken by the dense scrub brush and frequent mesquite trees. Despite the lack of cohesion, the battalion advanced, propelled forward by their NCOs and officers bringing up the rear of the advancing *soldados*. Will thought, "They're learning. Leading from just behind the line, the officers will exercise more control than when leading from the front. But it makes them harder to hit. What a shame."

As the infantry swept by the skirmishers, the *cazadores* ceased fire. Will shouted to Crockett, "David, how about one more volley and let's pull back!"

When the advancing infantry were four hundred feet away, Crockett sent one last bullet into the advancing line then called out, "Back to our next line!" Will joined the frontiersman as they raced back toward Seguin's cavalry. Glancing back at where they had been, Will saw one of his men down. It was clear from his position that he was dead. In the back of his mind, Will found it vaguely unsettling as he realized this campaign was inuring him to the casual death found on the battlefield.

Coming upon Seguin's Tejanos, Will waved to the wiry Tejano captain, "Juan, we're going to fall back a little ways. Send a man back to Grant and let him know we're leading at least one regiment straight into his position." Seguin sent a horseman galloping back to Grant's position on the Nueces while the remainder of his mounted troops moved toward their next fallback position.

The line of Mexican infantry couldn't move any faster than its slowest soldier, and the tangled growth of scrub brush covering the ground and the frequent mesquite trees slowed their advance even further.

Will knew few things are as difficult as a fighting retreat. After falling back a hundred yards, Crockett's men hurriedly reloaded before turning to fire on the Mexican battalion. Like a conductor, directing an orchestra, Crockett deliberately adjusted the pace of his retreat, allowing the advancing *soldados* to nip on the heels of his riflemen, but just out of effective range of their muskets. Will saw Crockett had things well in hand and turned to catch up to Seguin. Over the next ten minutes, the Texian riflemen and the Mexican line regiment played a deadly game of cat and mouse. The result was that Crockett and his men arrived at the Nueces River with the lead element of the Mexican army just a little more than hundred yards behind them.

Colonel Grant had allowed the two artillery officers latitude in how they positioned their artillery and they made the most of the previous four days. In addition to the dozen artillery pieces from the Alamo, they added to their defensive work the three cannons Will collected from Fannin's command. Two batteries with three cannon each covered the Camino Real where it intersected with the Nueces. Because the Nueces was little more than a shallow creek here, the artillery officers lined the other nine guns within a couple of hundred yards of the road, covering the southern bank of the river.

Remembering the effectiveness of Crockett's dedicated marksmen on the Rio Grande, Grant duplicated that with the riflemen under his command. He spread a hundred teams of three along the northern bank of the Nueces, over a width of more than two hundred yards.

Will sat atop his horse on the southern bank of the Nueces River, next to Captain Seguin. They watched Seguin's Tejano mounted troopers ride by, splashing across the shallow water of the ford. They galloped to the rear of the Texian line, passing by Colonel Grant, who stood opposite Will on the northern bank of the river.

Apart from Will and Seguin, Crockett's riflemen were

the only remaining Texians south of the Nueces now. Will speculated that the latest scattering of shots nearby announced Crockett's current position. No sooner had the thought formed in his mind than he watched a couple of dozen riflemen sprint down the road, splashing across the ford's foot deep water. Crockett, still afoot, paused by Will and Seguin and watched the last of his men splash across the chilly water.

After the last of their men reached the northern bank, Will reached down, offering Crockett a hand up. Along with Seguin, the two crossed the shallow waters, reaching the north side as the first Mexican troops arrived on the southern bank. A flurry of shots rang out as the Mexican infantry hastily fired at the three officers. Bullets buzzed around them and Will felt something slam into his horse. He tried using the reins to control the beast, but as the horse pitched to one side and fell, it threw the two men hard to the ground. Winded as he slammed to the ground, Will rolled to the side, tumbling into a rifle pit. He looked up, trying to catch his breath and saw several men kneeling in the trench, looking back at him, just as startled as he felt. A second later, Crockett fell in on top of him. Without missing a beat, the Tennessean drawled, "Well, boys, me and Colonel Travis thought we'd drop in on y'all and say our howdys."

The Mexican officers, following immediately behind their *soldados*, saw the narrow and shallow Nueces, and shouted for their men to hurry across. No sooner had the first Mexican infantryman stepped into the languidly flowing brook than a dozen bullets struck him and his companions. An instant later, the entire Texian side of the river was ablaze with rifle fire, sweeping dozens of *soldados* from their feet. An enraged shout erupted from the men of the *activo* battalion and with encouragement from their officers, they slogged across the shallow water.

The riflemen, from their entrenched positions, swapped weapons with their reloaders and swiftly fired again into the surging ranks of Mexican infantry, who ran, with bayonets fixed through the shallow water. They were barely more than halfway across the narrow waters when a third, more devastating volley swept the river clear of charging *soldados*.

A hazy pall of smoke hung low over the river as a lone Mexican infantryman splashed onto the northern bank, and as he looked behind him, he sagged when he realized he alone was left standing. Behind him, the waters of the Nueces ran red with the blood of his companions, those who had not fled back to the dubious safety of the scrub brush and mesquites through which they had passed just minutes earlier.

Will watched, from the rifle pit dug in the bank of the river, as to a man, the Texians held their fire. The lone *soldado* edged back into the river, and slowly retreated to the other side, never turning his back on his foes. In one of those peculiar moments in history, this lone survivor tested the edge of endurance and fortitude, was rewarded by his opponents with the one thing he still had to give, his life. Will would never find out who this lone *soldado* was, nor if he survived the battle, but in the years afterward, when soldiers got together and swapped tales of the Battle of the Nueces, the story of this lone survivor was often told.

As the men, in their cotton, white summer uniforms filtered away from the river, Will saw the banner of the Aldama battalion coming forward. He remembered their bravery from when they splashed across the Rio Grande a few days before. From where the flag fluttered in the chilly breeze, Will figured they were stopped a good distance from the river, but the dense brush and tree cover made it impossible to see clearly more than a couple of dozen yards beyond the southern bank of the river.

Two more banners came forward, representing the Toluca and the Zapadores battalions. It was impossible to gauge the size of the assembling force, as long as they remained behind the thick cover of mesquite trees. Minutes passed leaving Will to wonder if Santa Anna would try something different. It seemed to Will, the dictator was a slow learner, but he had learned to put scouts out ahead of his column. Will was uncertain of the dictator's next move. He told himself, "We're committed here, and second-guessing is counterproductive."

Finally, as Will's nerves started to wear, he heard bugles echoing from the Mexican line. Above the stubby mesquite trees, he watched the banners bobbing along and knew his questions were about to be answered. When the three battalions of advancing Mexican infantry were around a hundred feet from the river, the Texian riflemen began firing as they saw the advancing infantry through the dense cover of shrubs and trees. The trench was crowded with five men in it, but Will edged to the side where he could watch their front as Crockett stepped up beside him and fired at a target. The other three men fell into the role of reloaders, trading their loaded rifles to Crockett, for empty ones. Despite the heavy fire coming their way from the Texian line, the three battalions advanced at a run. The charging men understood they had to cross the river to close with the Texians and stop the murderous punishment.

When the lead elements of the Mexican battalions cleared the tree line, Will guessed he was looking at less than a thousand men. Even as officers and NCOs attempted to dress their ranks, the *soldados* ignored them as they ran, with their bayonetted muskets pointing toward the Texians. The average *soldado* wanted nothing to do with standing and trading shots with the deadly Texians. Those along the road ran down the sloping track into the water, while those on the flanks leapt down the banks, landing in the riverbed. Every few seconds a hundred bullets crashed into their ranks, tearing into soft flesh, maiming and killing dozens.

Will loosened his sword as he watched hundreds of *soldados* splashing through the shallow water toward their defenses. From behind him, he heard Captain Carey's distinctive voice shouting, "Battery A! Fire!"

To his left, Will heard the three closest cannons add their explosions to the staccato sound of rifle fire. He was staring at the surging Mexican line when three hundred bits of scrap iron and lead balls slammed into the rushing men. Will gawked, his mouth agape. It was like a scythe swept through the men, knocking scores of them off their feet.

Will thought it was like someone running headfirst into a solid door, as he watched the rushing Mexican force grind to a halt, as close to half their number were now thrashing in the shallow river or lying dead, their blood mixing with the languorous water as it flowed downstream. He barely had time to take in the shocked confusion on the survivors faces when the three cannons to the left of the ford swept the remaining *soldados.*

The sound of more artillery firing echoed from both flanks, as Will imagined a similar devastation wrecking the remnants of the three Mexican battalions. A bitter cloud of smoke clung to the river's surface, but dissipated quickly as a chilly northern breeze swept across the battlefield. To his immediate front, he saw no foe rise and flee southward, even though to both sides of the ford he could hear the sound of men running away.

Despite his years as a soldier, Will had never seen anything like this. He stared at the carnage along the river bed. At least at the Rio Grande, the river carried off most of the enemy casualties with the current, away from the battlefield. The Nueces didn't afford the dead and dying that courtesy. Along the shallows of the ford, where the water was less than a foot deep, he saw the bodies piled two and even three deep. Meandering downstream, the water flowed crimson along the entire breadth of the river, staining the shoreline. Will tried to maintain his composure as he felt a tear slide down his cheek. Along the length of the defensive line he heard cheers from his victorious soldiers. There was no joy for Will, seeing the mangled bodies clogging the shallow water. He felt a hand on his shoulder and saw Crockett from the corner of his eye. The frontiersman's expression was equally somber as he said, "Let 'em holler, Buck. They won a great fight today and gave Santa Anna a horrible bloody nose. The flower of Mexico may well have died here today. Our boys, they've earned it."

Chapter 12

The echo of the cheers from the Texian defenses still reverberated in Will's ears as he crawled from the crowded rifle pit. He looked across the Nueces as the remnants of the three battalions disappeared from view, hidden by the mesquite trees and scrub brush that lined the river. He glimpsed down at his jacket and saw it was covered with dirt from the pit. As Will knocked the dirt from his jacket, he saw Colonel Grant followed by Juan Seguin coming down the road, emerging from a defensive position, walking toward him.

From below, in the rifle pit, Will heard, "Buck, you got time to help an old man up or you going to stand there slack-jawed?"

After helping Crockett up from the rifle pit, Will greeted Grant and Seguin as they arrived. "Well done, Colonel Grant. That was well fought."

Grant smiled wearily, "Our men are the ones who earned the honors, Colonel Travis. But were it not for Colonel Crockett's idea for using our marksmen so effectively, I canna' say for certain that we'd have been as successful." In his thick Scottish brogue, he continued, "Let me lead the men in attacking Santa Anna's army now, while they're disorganized and confused."

Seguin jumped into the conversation, "Allow me and my men to lead the attack, Colonel Travis. We have earned the right to pay back Santa Anna for all he has done to the people of Texas and Mexico!"

"Seems to me that there's probably enough of ol' Santa Anna to go around." Crockett gently chuckled, good naturedly at the Tejano and Scotsman, and continued, "If y'all ain't done twisting his tail yet, then why don't we all go over yonder and remind him that he ain't Napoleon."

While the officers stood next to the rifle pit on the bank of the Nueces River, Will felt a heavy burden on his shoulders. The sleepless nights during the retreat were catching up to him, as he stifled a yawn. Every skirmish Will and Crockett had led was defensive and from behind cover. He knew Crockett and Seguin were suffering from the same fatigue, yet both were eager to come off the defense and attack.

Four years before, Will went the better part of a week on very little sleep during the chaos that defined the battle of Fallujah. This was no worse, he rationalized as he attempted to push through the exhaustion. To his right, Crockett looked back at him, with an expectant look. Quietly sighing as he struggled to get a handle on his exhaustion, Will turned to the Tennessean and asked, "What are your thoughts, David? Go on the offense or wait for Santa Anna?"

Crockett looked across the Nueces River, toward the location of the Mexican camp. He stared for a moment, as if he could see the retreating *soldados*, despite the dense brush and mesquites, "We got Santa Anna right where we want him at the moment. Up 'til now, we've been the greased pig and he's been the city slicker playing at farm work. Now, he's gone and hurt himself while wrestling this here pig. I reckon now is the time we learnt him a lesson; we're not just a greased pig but a greased boar. Our tusks are sharp and deadly."

Will knew that Crockett was every bit as tired as he, so he did his best to shake off the fatigue and said, "David, I believe you have the right of it. Let's get this done. Colonel Grant, instruct Dickinson and Carey to assemble their men as a reserve company. If we do this right, we'll be only a few minutes behind the Mexican retreat." Will fervently hoped there wouldn't be time for either side's artillery to play a role.

Instructing Grant, he said, "Take the men from Ward's battalion that are armed with muskets and have them form up a second reserve company." Disappointed to not lead the attack, Grant saluted and moved off to organize the men.

Juan Seguin had stood by, shifting from foot to foot while Will spoke with Grant. "What about my Tejanos, Buck? It's only right that we get in on this fight!"

"And you will, Juan. You're going to command our cavalry. Take your men, as well as the other mounted riflemen, split them up and cover both our flanks. Santa Anna still has the Dolores Regiment that we know of. Be careful. All these mesquite trees and prickly pear cactuses play to the infantry's advantage."

Seguin ran off to collect the mounted soldiers, leaving Will and Crockett standing alone, looking across the river at the tangle of mesquite and brush that separated the two armies. "I believe that's going to give you around four hundred fifty men, David. Same setup as before. I want one hundred fifty teams of three men each. I know you'll have a lot of muskets mixed in, so if we can, let's close to within a hundred yards of their camp and kick 'em while they're down."

A few minutes later, Seguin led his cavalry across the ford, threading though the brush and mesquites. He led half to the left flank of Crockett's men, while the other half took to the right. With sword drawn, Will walked beside Crockett, just behind their riflemen, where he watched those he could see, sort themselves into three-man teams, the best marksmen leading. He felt silly carrying the sword, but saw the approval in the stares of nearby riflemen. Behind him, Will heard the artillerymen, carrying muskets, following behind Colonel Ward and another sixty men.

It was difficult enough for Will and Crockett stepping around scrawny bushes and prickly pear cactuses, but it was clear that the same cluttered terrain which earlier slowed Santa Anna's attack now worked against the Texians, as they attempted to cross the same arid terrain.

Evidence of the Mexican battalions' retreat across the same ground just minutes before was everywhere, as Will stepped over a blue-jacketed body, likely a *soldado* from the Activo Toluca Battalion, who had succumbed to his wounds. Ahead, Will saw one of his riflemen pause as he came across a wounded *soldado*. The rifleman, clad in a buckskin hunting shirt, took his canteen, knelt by the injured *soldado*, and held the canteen to the other man's lips. In a way, as Will advanced with his men toward the Mexican army, he was reminded of the battle of San Jacinto. He recalled more than half the fatalities suffered by the Mexican army came after it was destroyed as a fighting force.

"David, let's not let things get out of control. I want our officers making sure that our boys take prisoners whenever possible."

Crockett nodded, "Good thinking, Buck. I recall a time or two in the Creek War, some of our boys let their blood get up and did things that no Christian ought to do."

Ahead of their advancing line, Will noticed the further away from the river they advanced, the less tangled the undergrowth and mesquites became. As the men in front of him broke through the mesquite, they paused. When he joined them, Will saw what drew them up. In the center of the field he saw the Mexican army had stopped setting up their camp as the broken men of the failed attack streamed back across the open field. Will had no doubt that the men milling around the camp were not expecting their compatriots to stream back in a state of disorder and shock. When the *soldados* in the camp realized Will's riflemen were hard on the heels of their retreating comrades, some started pointing toward the long, thin line of Texian riflemen. Will likened it to a child kicking an ant pile as the camp realized, for the first time since Santa Anna brought his Army of Occupation across the Rio Grande, the Texians were attacking.

Several men from the Dolores Regiment sprinted to their horses and in their haste, rode bareback toward the Texian line; their knees gripping their horses' flanks, as they lowered their lances at Seguin's flanking cavalry. In front of the camp, several officers and NCOs struggled to assemble their men into their companies and battalions. At the center of the encampment Will saw a couple of battle standards flying, around which several hundred men appeared to be galvanizing. But the shattered remnants of the Aldama, Toluca, and Zapadores battalions barely slowed down as they looked behind and saw the Texians hard on their heels. Will stared agape as some of the defeated *soldados* threw down their muskets to run all the faster.

Will recognized the two standards assembled in the center of the camp. They were the standards from the first day's battle. The blue-jacketed men of the Jimenez and Matamoros Battalions hurriedly dressed their ranks, their buglers urgently calling the rest of the Mexican army to arms.

General Almonte heard the crashing sound of gunfire a few hundred yards to the front of where his Excellency earlier ordered camp to be constructed. The field ran along the east side of the Camino Real, and apart from a few errant mesquite trees, was free from thick brambles and scrub brush so common in this part of Mexico. He was thoroughly sick of chasing the elusive company the army had dogged over the last four days. Every skirmish slowed them down and invariably cost lives, lives Almonte hated to see wasted.

Almonte jerked his head toward the river, a scant quarter mile away, when he heard the deep-throated roar of field artillery added to the cacophony of gunfire. He turned and saw their eight artillery pieces. He swore as it dawned on him what this meant, "Damn!" He thought, *"Those rebels we've been chasing ran us straight into their main army."*

He walked to the edge of the camp, looking to the north, as the sound of gunfire died away. One of the few remaining officers of the Jimenez Battalion joined him, "Sounds like General Cos has run into trouble, General. Shall I assemble the battalion?"

Almonte looked toward his Excellency's headquarters tent. Santa Anna was deep in a conversation with his new aide-de-camp and appeared to ignore the sounds of battle. He thought of approaching his Excellency and asking for permission, but as he looked to the north, he dismissed the idea and nodded to the young officer, and said, "Yes, Major Chavez, gather the men."

Almonte's focus was fixed on the ominous silence from the Nueces River. With a course of action now set, he found the captain commanding the remnants of the Matamoros battalion and told him to assemble his unit to the right of the Jimenez. He briefly considered finding Colonel Morales, but since the battle at el Rio Bravo del Norte, he thought Morales' men had been less diligent in their duties and desertions were high. As men broke from the tree line, streaming back toward the camp, Almonte set the thought aside and rushed to where Major Chavez was forming both regular infantry battalions to either side of their regimental standards. Maybe 250 men, Almonte figured.

The three battered battalions streaming back from their attack on the Nueces were not simply returning to the camp, beaten. They were looking over their shoulders and, it seemed to Almonte, running even faster. He glanced at his Excellency, who finally stopped talking to his aide-de-camp and was now yelling at the men who were streaming back into the camp, to stop and assemble. A few, Almonte noted, listened to Santa Anna, and stopped their flight, but others, babbling about the gates of hell being unleashed behind them, continued their headlong flight through the encampment.

The remnants from the Aldama, Toluca, and Zapadores battalions had not yet finished crossing the field when Almonte saw the protracted line of rough-looking infantry emerge from the tangled mesquite woods. He yanked his sword from his sheath and found Major Chavez standing between the two regular battalions of the Vanguard Brigade.

Looking to his right and left, Almonte despaired when he saw his line was scarcely more than fifty yards long. To the left of his truncated brigade, his spirits were buoyed as he watched more than a score of Mexican artillerists unlimbering their cannons and carrying ammunition from their caissons. From behind, he heard running feet and turned and saw dozens of men from the San Luis Potosi Battalion running forward, and adding themselves to his line. As he waited for the Texians to advance, he felt encouraged, knowing he and his men were not alone.

Less than two hundred yards separated the Texian riflemen from the Mexican camp. Will took a moment to watch the Mexican gunners rushing around their cannon, unlimbering the gun carriages from their caissons. While time was of the essence, he felt a nudge from Crockett as the frontiersman said, "Say something to the boys, they expect it."

As he stepped forward a few feet, he felt both silly and vulnerable as he raised his voice and shouted, "Men of Texas! I call on you in the name of liberty, patriotism, and everything that is dear to the American character to fight with me this day! The Lord is on our side! Victory or death!" As the men cheered, Will felt an overwhelming sense of pride as he returned to his place near Crockett.

"Not bad, Buck." Crockett practically shouted the words to be heard over the yelling of their riflemen. Will smiled sheepishly. He had borrowed a line from the letter penned by William B. Travis during the final days of the siege of the Alamo in a world now existing only in Will's mind. A look across the field showed the artillerists had decoupled their cannons from the caissons and were loading them.

"It's time," Will said to Crockett, pointing toward the cannons a couple of hundred yards away. The Tennessean stepped up to the line of riflemen, raised his rifle and sighted down the barrel. Will watched in fascination as Crockett held his breath then fired his rifle. Gunfire rippled up and down the line of marksmen. As soon as a sharpshooter fired, a reloader thrust a loaded rifle into his hands.

Will's attention stayed on the artillerymen, whose cannons could easily hit the Texian line with deadly canister fire or grapeshot. As he imagined the guns firing and tearing gaping holes in the Texian line, Will saw that his riflemen had similar fears as bullets struck several of the men attempting to load the Mexican field pieces. The Mexican infantry, to the right of the artillery, were loading their muskets as fast as they could, their officers screaming at them to hurry. Will guessed a couple of dozen men along the Mexican line had already fallen to the Texian marksmen when the line of Mexican infantry pointed their muskets and the line disappeared behind a wall of smoke as two hundred or more musket balls flew down range. The range was extreme for a musket, but Will saw a few of his men pitch backward, as they were struck. He was thankful that the volley was not more effective. Along the Mexican line the gun powder smoke quickly dissipated in the breeze, as the Texian marksmen picked off even more of the defenders.

The regular *soldados* of the Vanguard Brigade stood bravely against the aimed fire from the Texians for a few minutes. As the number of men still standing shrank, their ineffectual volleys fell silent and the remnants, with no officers still standing, turned and ran. Will thought now was the time to press the victory home. He stepped forward, and with his sword raised high, shouted, "For Texas and Victory! Charge!" His booted feet crashed into the dry soil as he raced across the field. A quick glance showed that nearly all the Texians were charging right behind him. But Crockett, with his rifle now in the crook of his arm, strolled leisurely behind the men, whistling a tune.

As he reached the remnants of the Mexican line, only a few *soldados* remained on their feet. Their weapons were scattered on the ground before them, but rather than simply flinging their arms into the air, that brave handful of men attempted to cover wounded comrades with their own bodies. This act of selfless courage reminded Will of the urgency to keep things from descending into blood-filled anarchy. He shouted at the top of his voice, "Round 'em up boys! If they surrender, take 'em prisoner!" As the Texians rushed over the few, huddled survivors along the Mexican line, the defeated *soldados* were battered to the ground, but left nursing the biting sting of defeat.

While most of the Texians rushed through the camp, Will saw two blue-jacketed *soldados* attend to a wounded officer, a sharp smell of iron filled his nose as he saw blood flowing freely from a head wound. The officer was dressed in a finely embroidered blue jacket over a white silk shirt. He was too young to be Santa Anna. In broken Spanish, Will asked, "Who is?"

With an air of resignation, one of the *soldados* replied, "General Juan Almonte."

Nodding at the Mexican *soldado*, Will heard the plaintive cries of the wounded. It was impossible to separate the injured from the dead by simply looking. Will guessed more than half the men from the Vanguard Brigade who tried to stand against Crockett's riflemen were able to fall back or surrender. To his left, Will saw several men from the Dolores Regiment fleeing on their horses, bareback, away from several of Seguin's cavalry. The Tejanos spurred their horses, galloping behind the lancers, pistols ablaze.

Crockett walked up, with Colonel Grant trailing behind. Following the two officers, marched Colonel Ward's men and their own artillerists, led by Captains Dickinson and Carey. Crockett nodded at Will, "Not bad, Buck, if I do say so myself. It looks like we may have bagged the whole passel of Santa Anna's army."

A fierce grin lit up Will's face as it sunk in; they had won a major victory. Crockett smiled in return, "What next, Buck?"

Will replied, "Get as many of our riflemen as you can, David. Let's figure out how many men have surrendered and how many wounded we'll need to take care of." Then, turning to Grant, Will pointed down the road. "Meet up with Seguin and his mounted men. Take him and his men along with all of your reserves. We need to get your companies and our cavalry down the road a far piece, and capture as many of the retreating Mexicans as we are able. If they regroup, let me know and we'll reinforce you."

As the sun set in the western sky, Will and Crockett sat in the large, spacious tent which previously belonged to Santa Anna. They were joined a short time earlier by Colonel Grant, who had burst into the tent and exclaimed, "We bagged the rest of his damned army, Colonel Travis!"

They pored over the reports flowing into the tent and as the afternoon wore on, the magnitude of the victory won slowly sank in on the assembled officers. The three regiments from the Operational Army's First Brigade that Santa Anna had sent chasing after Will's rearguard, had gone into battle with eight hundred men. Along the banks of the river more than a hundred men lay dead. Another eighty were dead within the Mexican Camp. Over three hundred were wounded once the camp had been secured. Two hundred were captured. The Vanguard Brigade was almost in as bad a shape. General Almonte's valiant attempt to protect the camp had resulted in more than forty killed. An additional thirty-five died throughout the camp. Almonte's brigade suffered around a hundred men wounded. More than three hundred were captured.

Will grimaced as he read the reports. Around two hundred fifty dead and more than four hundred wounded, in total. Will's little army captured between five and six hundred in addition to the wounded. "It's good that war is so terrible, lest we grow fond of it," Will said, borrowing a phrase from a world that would never be.

Crockett stood from the cramped camp stool, his back popping with age, "Truly, Buck. It was a terrible defeat we gave Santa Anna. Against only twelve of our own dead and a score more wounded, it's shocking."

Crockett was about to continue, when the tent flap was opened and Juan Seguin strode into the tent, pushing a tall Mexican in a plain blue infantry jacket. The man had dark-brown hair and fair skin. He arms were tied behind him. The expensive silk pants that the *soldado* wore looked starkly out of place compared to the coarse weave of the single-breasted, faded blue infantry jacket. Seguin's eyes shown bright in the reflection of lamp light, a look of triumph written on his face. He forced his captive into a camp chair across the table from Will and said, "Allow me to make introductions, Colonel William Barrett Travis and Congressman David Crockett, allow me to introduce you to *El Presidente* Antonio López de Santa Anna!"

Chapter 13

Will glared across the table, watching the Mexican dictator sulk, slouching in the rickety camp chair, while one of his elbows leaned on the stout table. Looking at the dictator, who was a couple of inches shy of six feet, Will was a little aghast by the calm demeanor affected by the man who in another world ordered the execution of hundreds of Texians. Will amended the thought as he looked down at Juan Seguin's translation of Santa Anna's orders, where hundreds of men had been executed in Zacatecas and Chihuahua on the dictator's orders.

Seguin sat at one corner of the table, reviewing piles of correspondence, setting aside those he intended to translate. Crockett paced along the back wall of the tent, casting frequent glances at their unperturbed prisoner. Will sat across from Santa Anna, shifting his eyes from the translated words to the exceedingly average looking man before him. "Well, General Santa Anna, what do you reckon we should do to you? Treat you like the butcher you are?" Will jabbed his index finger in his prisoner's direction, while holding the orders of execution with his other hand.

Santa Anna's demeanor shifted and he appeared uncomfortable as Will pointed across the table. However, when he replied, he spoke in a steady and calm voice, "I am simply the servant of the people and congress in Mexico City. I was charged to bring this army north and subdue rebellions within the republic of Mexico."

Crockett strode over to the tent flap, and flung it open, allowing the four men to see Texian riflemen guarding hundreds of prisoners. Crockett's harsh tone betrayed how troubled he was by Santa Anna's calm demeanor, as he pointed toward the prisoners, "How in the blazes is that working out for you, General?"

Will shared the Tennessean's frustration as the dictator replied with a casual shrug and said, "What we want and what we get are sometimes at odds with each other, Congressman Crockett."

Shaking his head, Crockett let the flap close. He returned to the table and looked down at the prisoner, "Why don't you answer Colonel Travis' question? Why shouldn't we shoot you and be done with it? Can you honestly say, you'd do things differently were the boot on the other leg?

Where Will's ire had not ruffled the dictator's feathers, Crockett's sharp words caused Santa Anna's calm veneer to crack, and for a moment, fear flickered across his face before being replaced by a nervous calm. Finding his voice, the dictator replied, "Why do something as imprudent as that?" He paused as he looked up searching for something in the frontiersman's eyes, "After all, you still need to negotiate with the legal government of Mexico. And at the moment, that government is sitting before you."

Will struggled to overcome the image that Hollywood had imprinted on his mind versus the reality of the slender, swarthy man in his early forties, sitting before him. What had been envisioned, influenced by popular culture, and what he saw were starkly different. Will was quickly learning, when reality bumped against what he knew from history, he needed to let go of history and accept reality. In this case, it was true in more than one way. If he spared Santa Anna's life now, then peace was within reach. "If it is to be as you say, Mr. President, then the first order of business is for you to order any troops already in Texas to leave and withdraw south of the Rio Grande, or as you call it, el Rio Bravo del Norte."

Santa Anna blanched at Will's demand. "But Tejas' border is here at the Nueces River. You would claim lands that rightfully belong to Tamaulipas, Coahuila, and Nuevo Mexico as your own?"

Will wagged his finger in Santa Anna's face, "How so, General? If you had your way, your border would have been the Sabine River. When you lose a war you rather have to give up what you'd rather not, or as you said earlier, sometimes what you want and what you get are at odds."

Santa Anna didn't like the taste of his words when thrown back in his face, and his chocolate-colored eyes blazed with intensity as his growled, "You have beaten me at the moment, Mr. Travis, but the balance of my army is only days behind me!"

Before Will could respond, Crockett put a hand on his arm, leaving his retort to die in his throat. "Seems to me, General," Crockett said, "that we can negotiate with you or we can negotiate with your successors in Mexico City. Do you think they'd give you a lovely state funeral with marching bands and pretty senoritas dressed in black to mourn their beloved and departed President?"

There was granitelike quality to Crockett's voice that drew the other men's attention like a lodestone, "Or negotiates with Texas a favorable treaty. Then return to Mexico and be president or dictator or whatever suits your fancy, if you can."

Will watched Santa Anna, while the dictator glared at Crockett. Before he responded, Santa Anna weighed Crockett's words, and drawing the same conclusion Will already had, bowed his head in defeat. "Congressman Crockett, you have the better of me at the moment. If you'll provide me pen and paper, I shall order Generals Gaona and Urrea as well as any other federal troops to return to south of el Rio Bravo del Norte."

Will stood on top of the chapel wall, watching the sun rise over the low walls of the Alamo on the 6th of March. He wore a grin larger than the one he wore after graduating from college, it seemed a lifetime ago. Never the most disciplined of armies, many of the six hundred men returning with him to San Antonio snaked through the gates of the Alamo into the large plaza with little military flair. Sandwiched between the jubilant Texians were more than five hundred Mexican prisoners, who could march under their own power. Some of the men from Ward's battalion were still a day behind as they escorted three hundred men whose wounds prevented them from keeping up.

From his perch atop the wall of the chapel, he watched several of his men escorting Santa Anna through the doors of the chapel where they locked him in the sacristy, a small room to the left of the doors of the nave. Except for the rooms off the main sanctuary, the chapel was open to the elements, never being completed since construction started in 1744. Will choked up as it dawned on him that today was the same day on which the Alamo fell in a world that would never be. Both he and Crockett were alive and well. Jim Bowie lay in the Alamo hospital, clinging to life, as disease ravaged his body. He was saddened to think that despite all the changes, Bowie's course appeared set.

In this new world, people would not revere the hallowed walls of the Alamo, what he grew up thinking of as the shrine of Texas liberty. Instead of San Jacinto, people would talk about the Nueces. Will smiled ruefully, thinking, *"Maybe in a hundred years they'll build an obelisk down there to celebrate our victory."*

Down in the chapel he saw the wrought iron door behind which Santa Anna now reposed and thought back to the day following the battle. They took Santa Anna's orders and sent General Castrillion to find General Urrea, who was marching north, along the gulf coast, to enforce Santa Anna's order for withdrawal. Colonel Mora was sent south, retracing the army's route along the Camino Real with Santa Anna's general order to retreat.

Before leaving the Nueces, Will sought volunteers for a ranging company, whose task would be to patrol the land between the Nueces and the Rio Grande. Everything he knew about the history of the Texas Revolution was now useless. It was imperative that a scouting force provide adequate time to react if the dictator's subordinate generals were less loyal than anticipated. Before the ink was dry on the orders authorizing the ranger company Will was confronted by Juan Seguin.

"Sir, I offer my services along with those of my men for the ranging company that you're recruiting."

Will had been expecting it. In another time, Will would have considered Seguin an adrenalin junky. "Juan, I appreciate your offer. And if I didn't have another assignment for you, your men are the first that I would have asked."

Seguin was intrigued, "What kind of assignment, Buck?"

Will explained, "Our citizens in the Bexar district are likely to be surprised by our victory, seeing as San Antonio has been traded back and forth between one faction or another since Mexico declared independence a quarter century ago. As we put the revolution behind us, it is important to the unity of our people that the Tejano face of San Antonio be unapologetically pro-Texas. Those politicians on the Brazos will declare independence any day now, and when that happens there can be no Centralist or Federalist voices, only a unified Texas voice."

Seguin scratched the stubble on his chin, considering Will's words with care. "What you say makes a lot of sense, Buck. In principal, I agree. But I want your guarantee that laws protecting Tejano rights along with Anglo rights won't just be on paper."

Will looked around the camp, as the two quietly talked, just outside the headquarters tent, and saw who he was looking for. He pointed toward the man, "Juan, if you want guarantees, then help me to see to it that Crockett rather than Houston or Burnet becomes the President."

Will grinned as he recalled Seguin's genuine smile.

The two had shaken hands and now that the army had returned to San Antonio, Juan and men were ideal apostles for Texas liberty.

Later in the morning on the 6th of March, Will sat in the office previously belonging to Colonel Neill, who had yet to return from a family emergency. Crockett sat across from him at the rough-hewn table. The Tennessean spoke first, "Do you figure that Grant has arrived at Washington yet?"

Will shrugged, "I hope so. It's been a week since he left for Washington from the Nueces. I'd love to be a fly on the wall when he walks into the convention and tells Sam Houston that the war's over, and we've won. And by the way, better get yourselves over to San Antonio before Colonels Crockett and Travis hammer out a treaty with Santa Anna."

Crockett's lips twitched upward, "Sam's alright, Buck. Even if he's in Andy Jackson's hip pocket, that don't make him a bad man. Hell, he was quite the hero back during the Creek War. But I done told you that I was only elected colonel of militia back in Tennessee because I brought more corn liquor on the election day. I'd prefer to think of myself as just a high private."

Will snorted derisively at the Tennessean. "David, that's pure balderdash. I haven't forgotten that you did more than your share in leading our men over the past couple of weeks."

Crockett shrugged noncommittally, "If I hadn't, you'd have done just fine on your own, Buck. You brought everything together. I still have a hard time imagining you crisscrossing south Texas, picking up Fannin and Grant and still meeting us on the Rio Grande, all in less than two weeks. That, my friend, is a special kind of leadership." Before Will could object, he continued, "How many men around here could have taken Fannin's regulars, Bowie's volunteers, and Seguin's Tejanos and forge them into a single fighting force that stopped the Napoleon of the West dead in his tracks?"

Will's face lit up at the praise. He thought Crockett was being generous. But it felt good that someone like the Tennessean, who Will highly esteemed, praised him so.

"What's next, Davy?"

Crockett scowled at Will. He didn't care for the nickname, but then he smiled, knowing Will meant it in playful fun. "Once Burnet and Houston find out that we've chased Santa Anna's army back into Mexico, they'll beat a trail to San Antonio. With any luck, they'll make their way here before they start trying to put a constitution together." He paused and thought for a moment before continuing, "I reckon I'll show up there and make sure that we take care of our famers and see to it the rich don't do to us what they're doing to our poor relations back east. Hell, maybe we can put a stick in ol' Andy Jackson's eye and get the British to recognize us first. That'd take the starch out of his shirt, sure enough." Crockett laughed at the mental image that he created. He became serious again, "What about you, Buck? You'd make a hell of an officer, I do believe."

Since the victory a week previous, Will had been thinking about what was to come. He decided if he could trust anyone, it would be Crockett. "If I can carve out a place here in the army, I will, David. But like you, I'd like to help with the constitution. I heard tell that Burleson was hot to make sure that folks can't go about freeing their slaves."

Hearing that, Crockett's expression hardened. "That

don't hardly seem fair. I ain't saying that I'm for or against owning a negro, Buck, but if a man's of a mind to set his slave free, who's to stop him?"

Will slid a glance at Crockett, "I suspect you heard that I already freed Joe. I still need to get the papers filed at the Casas Reales in Bexar, but I'm done with it. David, if Texas means anything to me, and you have to know it's true, it should mean that whether you were born a Tennessean or Alabaman, a Mexican or Scotsman, even a Cherokee or a negro, it should stand for the liberty of all of us."

Crockett sat on the opposite side of the table, quiet after Will's outburst. After what seemed an eternity to Will, he said, "Buck, I own that you're right. I have long thought that when we know what is right we should go ahead and do it. And damned if you're not right. When I was in Congress, I saw men happy to spend other people's money, but they were tighter than a virgin's, ah, well, you know, with their own." Both men smiled sheepishly at the word left unspoken. "But rest assured, after those years in Washington, working with my fellow Southerners, I know they aren't going to easily or freely give up on our particular institution, least ways, not overnight."

Will grinned slyly at Crockett and replied, "I happen to know a certain Tennessean that has just helped to win this here war. If he were to, who knows, maybe run for the office of, oh, I don't know, the presidency, he might be in position to begin to do something about it."

Crockett laughed at that. "Oh, Buck, from your lips to the Almighty's ears!" Will stood and grabbed a dented, tin cup and raised it to his friend, "To President Crockett of the Republic of Texas!"

Chapter 14

Will gazed into the clear, blue sky, looking beyond the stately oak tree growing in the middle of the church's cemetery. The weather, in typical Texas style, was unpredictable and the 8th of March was a fine day for a funeral, Will thought with no little morbidity. In the quiet moments, when the pressures of command allowed, he puzzled over the changes his actions set in motion. Even though Santa Anna sat in a cell in the chapel and the Alamo remained unconquered, Jim Bowie had succumbed to the disease that ravaged his body for the last two weeks. Will suspected Bowie's death was unavoidable when considering the knife fighter's long running battle with alcoholism, hard living and the abysmally harsh weather of the past month. Two nasty cold fronts had hammered south Texas and Bowie, like Will had endured them without the benefit of shelter. Even so, it was difficult for him to watch the casket being lowered into the consecrated ground of the church cemetery.

The priest's intonation in Latin meant little to Will, but as he stood in the cemetery, he was struck by how many of his soldiers had walked or ridden into San Antonio to watch the beloved commander of volunteers laid to rest, next to his wife, who had passed away a few years earlier. As Will scanned the crowd, ignoring the priest's words, he was also struck by how many of San Antonio's finest families turned out to say their last farewell. The crowd in the cemetery was about half Tejano and half Anglo-American. Will mused about how adroitly Bowie had navigated effortlessly through both cultures. Will was sure there was a lesson to be learned there from the hard-drinking knife fighter.

After the Priest concluded the service, a squad of nine men from Bowie's Volunteers marched up to the grave. The first three men stepped forward and fired a crisp volley into the air. A moment later, the next set of three stepped forward and fired another volley. Finally, the last set joined their companions, next to the grave and fired a final volley into the air. As the breeze scattered the gun smoke, many of the people in attendance filed by the grave, saying a last goodbye to a friend and hero.

After retrieving his horse, Will guided the mount over next to Crockett, who had attended the service too, and accompanied the Tennessean as they headed out of town, toward the Alamo. "You know, David, had it not been for Jim's death, everyone would still be celebrating the news from Washington-on-the-Brazos yesterday." The soldiers from the Alamo had filled the cantinas and saloons the previous night celebrating the declaration of independence signed on the 2nd of March.

Crockett nodded and matched his horse's speed to Will's until they crossed the Alameda Street bridge. Within sight of the Alamo, he turned and said, "Buck, after everything that has happened over the last few weeks, you should know, all of Bowie's volunteers will follow you to hell and back."

This wasn't something which had crossed his mind until now. Most of Will's energy since capturing Santa Anna was spent getting enough supplies to feed both his army and the prisoners. He thought about it and replied, "You may be right, David. Truth be known, I'd be more than happy if they'd just get it out of the way and elect you to be their colonel.

Crockett shook his head, "No, thank you. I doubt I could scare up enough corn liquor here in Bexar for me to buy enough of their votes, and most of the boys ain't partial to tequila. As the Almighty is my witness, Buck, I hope it isn't necessary either. Sam and the rest of the government ought to be here within a week. Once they're here we can get us a treaty from ol' Santa Anna, one we've earned."

Will noticed, and not for the first time, when Crockett wanted to, he had an excellent grasp of proper English. When he pointed this out, Crockett laughed and replied, "Buck, I was so wet behind the ears when the folks from Tennessee sent me to Washington City back in twenty-one, that I couldn't have told you a dinner fork from a dessert fork. But I read a lot and got invited to more fancy parties than I care to count. I guess all that dandifying paid off."

Chuckling at Crockett, Will asked, "So, all that rough frontier garb and talk is just an act?"

Crockett chuckled in response, as they approached the Alamo, "Hell, no. It's all that highfalutin talk that's the act."

On the afternoon of the 11th of March Will stood on the steps leading to his headquarters, watching a company from the New Orleans Greys stand at attention in the Alamo Plaza, in two parallel lines by the gatehouse. The captain commanding the company snapped a crisp salute as General Sam Houston rode through the gate at the head of a company of mounted riflemen. As Houston swung out of the saddle, Will strode across the plaza and drew up before the commander of the army of Texas and saluted. "General Houston, welcome to the Alamo, sir."

Houston returned the salute, "Colonel Travis, your men look very well." He paused as he looked at the uniformity of the Greys and nodded again. "I must congratulate you, sir. You and your men performed beyond my highest expectations down on the Nueces."

Will noticed that Houston's jaw clenched when he spoke. From William B. Travis' memories, Will knew Houston had arrived in Texas just the previous year, and had angled for command of the military during the battles in 1835. Will's view from history books was more favorable than Travis' memories, but even so, it was evident Houston's ambition was boundless. He served as governor of Tennessee when he was only thirty-six years old. Now, seven years later, Will knew Houston aspired to an even higher position. He suspected that Houston felt cheated out of the recent victory.

The moment passed, and Will saw that Houston was relaxed as he asked, "Where's he at? Take me to see *el Presidente*."

Will escorted Houston through the smaller chapel courtyard then into the chapel where the dictator was still under guard in the sacristy. Houston stood in front of the door, looking at Santa Anna, who sat at a small camp table. The dictator set the book he had been reading down and stood, nodding at Sam Houston, but otherwise remained silent.

Houston seemed unperturbed by the prisoner's calm demeanor as he said, "In a few days, General, members of our government will be arriving here in Bexar and we'll see what kind of treaty we can come up with. I'm certain you're ready to return to Mexico."

Santa Anna's eyes stayed glued on Houston's as it appeared that the dictator was taking the measure of the tall Texian general. When he spoke he was quiet, and Will had to lean in to hear him, "Hah, as if I had a choice in the matter, General Houston. I've no doubt you'll require everything of me that young Colonel Travis has won on the field of battle. But will you be able to keep it?"

With a casual, nonchalant shrug, Houston said, "We'll have a treaty, first, General. The rest is for tomorrow."

As Will led Houston out the chapel and up the stairs to his office above the hospital, Houston told him, "They'll need places to stay in town, Colonel Travis, but you should know the entire provisional government will arrive here over the next few days. There are more than three hundred fifty soldiers behind me and I want you to find a place to billet them in or around the Alamo. We're going to make sure that the city is safe for the negotiations."

As Will offered Houston his chair in the office, Houston asked, "Now, I heard tell that my old friend Congressman Crockett was here. Would you mind sending for him?"

Sam Houston was a mess of contradictions, Will had decided, as he, Will, Grant, and Seguin met in the small office over the next several days. At times Will felt Houston was jealous and at other times, he was even-tempered and considerate when interacting with Will. The current meeting, fortunately for Will, was the latter.

Grant was talking, his Scottish brogue unmistakable, "But General Houston, we've destroyed two entire brigades of Santa Anna's army. I'm certain we could seize Coahuila and add it to Texas."

Houston didn't try to hide a theatrical sigh, "Damnit Grant, I've told you before, that dog won't hunt. We risk biting off more than we can chew just claiming everything down to the Rio Grande. If you want to go off to Coahuila by your lonesome, I'm not going to stop you, but neither am I going to come to your rescue."

Will was tired of Grant's persistent demands that the army of Texas, which now numbered more than a thousand men, should go gallivanting into northern Mexico. As Grant sputtered, Will said, "How likely are we to get Santa Anna to give us El Paso del Norte?" He pointed to a spot on the map, almost six hundred miles west of San Antonio. His finger traced the Rio Grande up to where Santa Fe was stenciled on the map and continued, "Let alone Santa Fe and Albuquerque?"

Houston smiled predatorily, "Colonel Travis, we have Santa Anna bent over a barrel. He'll give us anything we ask for. We'll insist that they give up New Mexico east of the Rio Grande all the way up to the headwaters."

Will was thinking that Houston's ambitions were a

pipedream when Crockett spoke up, "Sam, you're right, we have Santa Anna between Scylla and Charybdis. But can you tell me that he won't be deposed when he gets back to Mexico City with his tail between his legs?"

Will was perplexed by the idiom about Scylla and Charybdis. He had never heard the expression before, but Travis' memory filled in the blank. It was an idiom from classical Greek, basically between a rock and a hard place. His opinion of Crockett, already high, climbed even higher.

Houston replied, "David, like as not, you're right. It won't surprise me if he gets deposed the first day he steps back across the Rio Grande, but this gives us two things we desperately need. The first is time. It's going to take Santa Anna's successors two or three years at the least before they can send any kind of force north of the Rio Grande. And second, when they do, it will give us a firm casus belli to march out there and take them by force and in accordance with this here treaty, which we will honor. And that's one of the other reasons, Colonel Grant, that we're not going to incite Mexico against us further today over any claims you might think we have in Coahuila."

Will's head was pounding. The negotiations with Santa Anna probably would be easier, he thought, if there were fewer cooks in the kitchen. When David Burnet, the interim President, arrived on the 16th of March, Will expected him to appoint commissioners to negotiate a treaty with Santa Anna. Burnet spurned the idea when Sam Houston suggested it. That led to a screaming match between the two men in the Alamo plaza, witnessed by much of the army of Texas.

Lorenzo de Zavala was Burnet's acting vice president which was why Will stood next to Juan Seguin, listening to the cavalry officer plead with the older Mexican on the 16th. "Señor Zavala, thank you for taking the time to speak to me and Colonel Travis. You must intercede with President Burnet and see if he'd agree to lead a three-man commission. Surely you can see that everyone's interests would be best served if President Burnet, Congressman Crockett, and yourself were the ones to negotiate with the dictator."

Zavala was a cagey politician and had already been wearing down Burnet's resistance. When he suggested Crockett's inclusion, the provisional president caved and added the Mexican and Tennessean as commissioners along with himself.

The negotiations were held in the long barracks, after Zavala had convinced President Burnet that including Crockett as a commissioner would be viewed favorable by most people in Texas. Almost as an afterthought Zavala mentioned that the Tejanos would feel they were part of the revolution if their interests were also included, so Burnet added Zavala to the third seat at the negotiations.

Now, a couple of days after the negotiations started, Will fantasized about aspirin as his head threatened to erupt. *"What in the hell was I thinking,"* Will thought, *"I should have negotiated with Santa Anna myself and been done with it before the government arrived."* Instinctively he knew the reason, but it still felt better to think otherwise. Will shuddered to think what time would do to Texas if he, as part of the military, ignored the dictates and interests of the civilian government. *"Seems that's how Mexico got stuck with Santa Anna."*

He irreverently thought.

The negotiations for the day were over, and he sat in a cantina, across the main square in San Antonio with Crockett and Burnet eating a meal of tamales and beans. Will scowled at Burnet after reading the first draft of the treaty, "Can you please explain to me why we're requiring Santa Anna's forces to give back any slaves that they might have captured? Hell, the latest news from Refugio is that when General Urrea left there he didn't have any with him. Why are you throwing a bone to a few slave owners, Mr. President?"

Burnet set his fork down, and glared back at Will, "You mean like you, Colonel Travis?"

Will reminded himself for what seemed like the hundredth time not to underestimate anyone that he talked to. Someone with a nineteenth century view of the world, like Burnet, was just as capable and intelligent as he was. And if he were honest with himself, as he glanced at Crockett, many were much smarter. Will sighed, "Mr. President, I have freed my man, Joe. It remains only to file in the courts here in Bexar when they resume. Hopefully soon."

Despite feeling weary holding a conversation with Barnet, Will thought he saw a slight nod of what might be approval from the other man. Barnet replied, "Listen, Colonel, many of our biggest supporters both here and back east expect, no, they demand that we support slavery. Between the three of us, I think it noble you freed your slave. However, you fight them at your own peril. There's a fine line between bravery, which you have a plenty, and stupidity. We cannot bite the hands that feed us, Colonel Travis, we have many bills to pay and they are the source of our money."

Head still pounding, Will massaged his temple. This

wasn't going the way he imagined it would go. "Mr. President, I'm not blind to the reality of our situation. While I may not like these obligations, I do understand them. Even so, can we not take the reference to returning any slaves and inserting language for compensation in its place? I would imagine that our beloved slave masters would rather have gold than an unhappy and unruly servant. It's not like there'll be any claims."

Burnet's dour look faded into a wide smile as he laughed, "Don't think that there won't be a line of claimants, Colonel. Every planter who has had a slave hand run off since the start of the revolution will line up to press their claims. But I take your meaning and I think your argument valid enough that it will satisfy our benefactors." He paused as he thought about Will's suggestion. After a long moment he raised his hands in mock surrender, "Fine. We can insert the language that requires the Mexicans open up a consulate here in Texas to adjudicate any claims. Will that smooth your feathers, my young eagle?"

Will nodded. "It's the best of available options, sir. How long before you figure Mexico will open that consulate?"

Burnet looked back and forth between him and Crockett and replied, "Sometime around the time that Gabriel blows his horn. But, listen, Colonel Travis. I can see like a recent convert, your passion burns bright against the South's peculiar institution, but be careful you don't get burned. As a native of New Jersey, I have long supported the suppression of the trade, and that's probably why, when we're done drafting the constitution I won't have a chance standing for election. But Congressman Crockett here, as one of the heroes of the day, his chances are excellent. If you want to change things then you need to change the trajectory of Texas. To do that, it helps to win elections and set policies."

Will stood on top of the Alamo's gatehouse, watching as Santa Anna was escorted from the fort by a company of Will's regular cavalry. They would escort him to the small port town of Copano, where a United States flagged ship was waiting to take him back to Mexico. He had been released and was taking the Mexican copy of the treaty with him. Will wasn't sure the government back in Mexico City would even allow the dictator to set foot in Vera Cruz, let alone consider the terms of the treaty.

He glanced down at a copy of the current issue of the *Telegraph and Texas Register*, where the terms of the treaty were published. He leaned against the outer wall and reread the newspaper's summary of the treaty;

T.R.Borden, publisher, San Antonio de Bexar, Republic of Texas

The treaty was entered on the 23rd March 1836 between his Excellency David G. Burnet, interim President of the Republic of Texas of the one part & His Excellency General Antonio López de Santa Anna President General in Chief of the other part.

The first Article

General Antonio López de Santa Anna agrees that he will not take up arms nor will he exercise his influence to cause them to be taken up against the People of the Republic of Texas during our war of Independence.

The second Article

All hostilities between Mexico and Texas and their

troops will cease on both land and water.

The third Article

All Mexican troops will evacuate the territory of Texas passing to the other side of the Rio Grande del Norte, also known as Rio Bravo del Norte in Mexico.

The fourth Article

The Mexican Army shall not take the property of any person without his consent & just indemnification, using only such articles as may be necessary for its subsistence during its retreat. In any case when the owner may not be present notification shall be made to the Commander in Chief of the Army of Texas or to the Commissioners to be appointed for the adjustment of such matters an account of the value of the property consumed, if the name of the owner can be established.

The fifth Article

That all private property including cattle, horses, that may have been captured by any portion of the Mexican Army shall be restored to the Commander of the Texian Army or to such other persons as may be appointed by the Government of Texas to receive them. Any citizen of the Republic of Texas may file for recompense of claim for their negro slaves or indentured persons that may have been captured by any portion of the Mexican Army or may have taken refuge in the said army since the commencement of the late invasion. The Mexican government shall establish a consulate in the largest city of the republic where claims may be adjudicated.

The sixth Article

The troops of both armies will refrain from coming into contact with each other & to this end the Commander in Chief of the Army of Texas will be careful not to approach within a shorter distance of the Mexican Army than fifteen miles (five leagues).

The seventh Article

The Mexican Army shall not make any other delay on its march than that which is necessary to take up their hospitals baggage & cross the rivers - any delay not necessary to these purposes to be considered as an infraction of this agreement.

The eighth Article

By Express to be immediately dispatched, this agreement shall be sent to Gen'l Filisola & to Gen'l Samuel Houston, Commander of the Texian Army in order that they may be apprised of its stipulations & to this they will exchange engagements to comply with the same.

The ninth Article

That all Texian prisoners now in possession of the Mexican Army be forthwith released & furnished with free passports to return to their homes in consideration of which a corresponding number of rank & file now in possession of the Government of Texas shall be immediately released -- The remainder of the Mexican prisoners that continue in possession of the Government of Texas to be treated with due humanity any extraordinary comforts that may be furnished them to be at the charge of the Government of Mexico.

The tenth Article

Gen'l Antonio López de Santa Anna will be sent to Vera Cruz as soon as it shall be deemed proper --

This treaty was signed in San Antonio de Bexar this 23rd day of March 1836 by David G. Burnet and Antonio López de Santa Anna

Chapter 15

17th March 1836

From the small confessional room, to the side of the Chapel's nave, Will listened to Santa Anna's footsteps in the sacristy, next door, where the dictator paced back and forth. He felt more than heard Crockett come up behind him, as he stood staring at stacks of woven baskets filled with cornmeal and wheat flour along the walls of the little room. From behind, Will heard, "Buck, I heard tell that Houston's got some more wagons coming from Columbus with more food in the next few days. I reckon we're well supplied with vittles."

Will looked behind him and saw Crockett standing just in the doorframe of the confessional. "Ah, just the man I was looking for. Close the door and join me." After closing the door to the room, Crockett stepped over next to Will. Behind a row of baskets, there was a narrow space. Laying in the cavity, on the floor, was a lockbox.

Crockett's eyebrows raised in surprise. His voice was low when he asked, "Now, Buck, what have you got there?"

From around his neck, Will drew a cord from which dangled a brass key. The light from a narrow window reflected off its polished surface. With the key in hand, Will knelt in front of the box. After inserting it into the lock and turning, he heard a satisfying click and the box was unlocked. Will flipped the lid back, opening the box. A sizable pile of gold coins gleamed in the weak light from the narrow window.

Crockett whistled appreciatively. "Bless my soul, Buck. My, how you have kept your powder dry, boy."

Will quietly chuckled, as the image of Santa Anna pacing in the room next door came briefly to mind. "Well, I noticed this little footstool in Santa Anna's headquarters tent, and well, his Excellency didn't have any need for the tent anymore, I was pretty sure he didn't have any use for this little footstool either."

Crockett helped Will drag the box from its hidden nook. He knelt beside Will and picked up a coin. It was a gold Spanish doubloon. "Any idea how much is here?"

Will nodded. "There's about seventeen thousand dollars in gold and another eighteen thousand dollars in silver, below the gold."

Crockett tunelessly whistled as he picked up a few coins and examined them. He stopped whistling as he bit a golden coin. He nodded, "Those are no fakes, Buck. But why, pray tell, haven't you told our august and noble President Burnet about this here find, or even General Houston?"

Will dramatically sighed, and with an air of theatrics said, "I was saving this news to tell the next president. You know the one, the one we'll be electing after we nail down our constitution." Will paused, letting the tension build until he continued, "But seeing as I figure that he's right here beside me, I thought I would go ahead and tell him now."

The Tennessean shook his head, chuckling. "Buck, don't be counting those chickens before they're hatched. I dare say that if our illustrious army commander has anything to say about it, I'll be sitting on my porch, in a rocking chair, smoking a pipe while waiting for the Almighty to come and take me home."

Shrugging, Will replied, "Maybe so, David. But he's not the hero of the Battle of the Rio Grande or of the Nueces, either. That, my coonskin-cap-wearing-friend, is you."

Crocket lowered the lid and Will locked the chest. As they pushed it back behind the baskets, the Tennessean replied, "That's mighty Christian of you, sharing all of that glory with me, Buck. But if I recall correctly, I wasn't the onlyiest one there."

Will gave his companion a lopsided grin as he replied, "While that may be true, I'm a long way away from thirty-five years of age. I doubt I'll be eligible once we're done putting a constitution together. If I'm lucky the only plum that I'll be able to pluck from the tree is command of the regular army."

Locking the door as they exited from the confessional room, Will nodded to the guard standing watch over the sacristy. When they exited the chapel Crockett finally replied, "Buck, if I decide to run against Sam for the presidency, I suspect that I know exactly who'll be my first choice to command the army. Now, you haven't kept this quiet for no reason, what have you been scheming about with all this gold?"

Will's eyes gleamed as he said, "Guns, David. I've been thinking that between the Mexicans to our south and Comanches to our west and north, we need the best guns that this money can buy. I recall hearing about an inventor back east, by the name of Colt. As I understand it, he's invented a revolving pistol that can fire several rounds before it needs to be reloaded. If we can get these pistols into the hands of our ranging companies and cavalry troops, it could help tip the balance back in our favor against the Comanche, if we can't get them to stop raiding our settlements by diplomatic means."

The image of a Ranger standing his ground, firing round after round at charging Comanches put smiles on both their faces. They walked across the fort's plaza and watched an engineer surveying the ground for a new wall to replace the crumbling northern wall. Will had obtained permission from Houston for the Alamo's expansion. Watching the engineer set up a ranging pole, Crockett said, "Buck, build up a little support among the delegates then send that letter to Mr. Colt." He fell silent as they watched the engineer work. A moment later, he continued, "There's someone else to whom you should also write. Back when I was in Congress, during the last session, I recall an appropriation bill for a gun that was being manufactured at Harper's Ferry. It was designed for a regiment of dragoons that the US government was recruiting for frontier service. If I recall correctly, the inventor's name is Hall. I believe that he's the ordnance officer at Harper's Ferry."

Will's curiosity was piqued, "What makes the gun special?"

"The gun's a breechloader. It's faster by a country mile to load than my ol' Betsy, and just as accurate if Hall's reports were true. Imagine what you could do with a rifle like that."

Will was speechless. He hadn't realized breechloaders were being made by the US military prior to the Civil War. He found his voice and replied, "David, with a gun like that on the Rio Grande, we wouldn't have needed to have two loaders for every marksman! It would be a real force multiplier."

Crockett nodded, "Force multiplier, hmm, that's a pretty turn of a phrase. We'd have a real leg up against Mexico and the Comanche. You should write Mr. Hall a letter too, while you're at it. I don't want to presume much, but should I win, I'll give you cover for the gold and silver if it ever came out that you have it."

18th of April 1836
To the honorable Samuel Colt,
Principal of Patent Arms Manufacturing,

Recently I heard of your trip to England where I understand you patented a revolving pistol, that you now seek to patent in the United States. Your design has garnered much attention in the army of the Republic of Texas, given its multiple firing capacity. In our ongoing war with the fierce and determined warriors of the Comanche nation, on our western frontier, we have paid a heavy price in both dead and captured because of the common limitation of our single shot muzzle loading rifles. I am writing to you directly, to request a purchase of pistols for our mounted ranger patrols, and have been authorized by the Government of the Republic of Texas for an initial purchase of 200 of your excellent pistols, as well as to inquire about licensing costs associated with locally manufacturing replacement parts. Please forward with all haste, the price of procurement of these pistols and related licensing costs and we will make payment once the order is ready for shipment to the Port of Galveston, Republic of Texas.

Your Servant,
Colonel William Barret Travis, commanding, Alamo,
San Antonio, Bexar, Texas.

Will observed the brass eighteen-pounder artillery piece, situated on the bastion atop the southwest corner of the fort. It was well polished and brilliantly reflected the noonday sun. Captain Carey sat on a stool, reading a book, while Joe, Travis' former slave, stepped back from the cannon, admiring his work. Walking up the incline to the bastion, it crossed Will's mind that in nearly every way, more than two months since he found himself in William B. Travis' body, he considered himself and Travis to be one and the same. It was easier on his mind to accept the different, conflicting memories without dwelling much on it anymore. Except in one area. When Will thought of Joe, it was always 'Travis' slave', and never 'my slave'. No matter how many times he examined Travis' memories, when it came to slavery there was simply too great a disconnect for his twenty-first century mind to accept.

Will considered himself pragmatic and knew he wasn't going to change things writ large today, but now that the city government was functioning again, he could do something about Joe. When Captain Carey saw him walking up the ramp he closed his book, stood and saluted Will. "Colonel Travis, sir."

Will returned the salute and replied, "The gun looks good, Captain." He glanced down on the stool and saw the title on the book, it was "*A Treatise on the Science of War and Fortifications*." Will's observation of Carey during the previous campaign was that he was a serious student of his duties, and he was pleased to see the officer reading a book which would deepen that knowledge. Will pointed to Joe and said, "I've some business in town and I need Joe to accompany me. How has he performed his duties?"

Carey looked at the polished barrel and replied, "I confess, Colonel Travis, that I was surprised when Colonel Neill told me you planned to manumit your property after the campaign and asked that I find a place for him in my battery. But he has been diligent in the duties to which he has been assigned, Colonel. I have found no fault with him."

Will nodded then said to Joe, "We've got business to attend to. Are you finished?"

Joe nodded, and dropped the rag into a small bucket by the gun before joining him at the ramp. Will turned back to Carey and said, "I commend you on your choice of reading material, Captain."

Carey smiled and replied, "Thank you, Colonel Travis. Not being a West Point graduate, I am doing what I can to learn the science of war."

After leaving the bastion, Will mounted his horse and handed the reins of a borrowed mount to Joe. The former slave ventured a question, "Where we going, Marse William?"

"To town. We've got business to conduct, and please, stop calling me Master. You're a free man, Joe. Today, we're going to make it official."

As they crossed the half mile between the Alamo and the main plaza in San Antonio, Will asked, "Did Captain Carey treat you fairly, Joe?"

"I reckon so," Joe said, "He didn't beat me or yell at me or anything like that."

"What did he have you do, while you were assigned

to his battery?"

"I polished the brass cannons, tended to the horses while we was down south, and cooked for the officers, sometimes."

While not what Will wanted to hear, it didn't surprise him. Will liked Captain Carey, because he was brave, considerate of his men, and was willing to learn how to better do his job. But as a native of Virginia though, Will found Carey's views on slavery to be … uncomplicated, as was the case with most of the people with whom he interacted.

Will guided his horse across the main square in San Antonio, to a low, single-story building housing the city government. Tying the horses to a hitching post in front of the building, Will led Joe into the office of the *Sindico Procurador*.

Manuel Martinez's job was a cross between city attorney and justice of the peace. After talking with Lorenzo de Zavala, Will learned Martinez was allowed to remain in the position until the new city and county governments were established. He reckoned it didn't hurt that Martinez was good friends with Jose Navarro, one of several Tejanos, elected to attend the constitutional convention. Navarro originally had been one of two Tejanos selected to attend the constitutional convention. The provisional government's decision to relocate to San Antonio, to conduct the treaty with Santa Anna had also caused the convention to move to San Antonio as well. Will figured it boded better for Tejano representation to have the constitutional convention here.

He pulled from his faded blue jacket a packet which he placed on Martinez's desk. When the Tejano looked up, he was startled to recognize Colonel Travis standing before him. Inwardly, Will smiled as the short man, with a swarthy complexion, stood, "My pardon, Colonel Travis. I was not aware that you would be coming by today. How may I be of assistance, sir?"

Will flipped open the packet and retrieved the bill of sale Travis had received when he bought Joe in 1834. He also unfolded a letter he had written back in February, before the campaign started, in which he freed Joe. Spreading them before the *Sindico Procurador*, he said, "The first of these is the bill of sale, showing where I purchased Joe here a couple of years ago. The second is a letter that I wrote, in which I freed Joe."

Martinez picked up both documents and examined them at length. After a few minutes, the Tejano official said, "Colonel Travis, your documents are in good order. I presume you wish to conclude this business today?"

Will nodded, "Of course, Señor Martinez. There's no time like the present to win one's freedom, wouldn't you agree."

Martinez's lips twitched into a ghost of a smile, catching the words' double meaning. "As you say, Colonel. I will draw up the manumission contract. If you do not have a witness, I will have someone from the alcalde's office serve as a witness. The *ayuntamiento* fees are still being collected, Colonel. The notarization of all forms is two pesos, or comparable United States currency."

Will chuckled. It was just like the alcalde, Francisco Ruiz to make sure Bexar's taxes were being collected.

Will agreed to return in an hour to collect the documents, after leaving payment with the *Sindico Procurador*. From there, he and Joe crossed the plaza, in the shadow of the church of San Fernando and entered a nearby cantina. While they ate, Will noticed another diner looking their way. The man was tall and thin with sandy hair. As Will and Joe finished their meal, the other man came over to their table.

Glancing up, Will saw the sandy-haired man was nearly as tall as he was. "Can I help you?" Will asked. His tone made the question sound like a statement. He didn't care for the looks the other man had been sending their way.

"You Colonel Travis?"

"Last time I checked, yes," Will replied dryly. "Who wants know?"

Without offering his hand, the sandy haired man said, "The name's Maverick, Sam Maverick. I heard tell that you were going to free your nigger."

Not caring for Maverick or his tone, He stood, looked the other man in the eye. "What of it? I haven't spent the last two months fighting to free Texas from the heels of a Mexican despot just to be told that I can't do with my property what I want."

Maverick glared back at Will, "You make it sound all noble, Colonel. And I don't rightly reckon that I'd stop you from doing with your property what you will, but you see, there's cause and effect, and that's what worries me about you."

Will cocked his head as he maintained eye contact with Maverick. "What do you mean cause and effect?"

"You free your nigger today and then tomorrow or maybe next year, you'll be telling the rest of us that we can't bring our slaves into Texas," Maverick said.

"Boy's smarter than he looks." Will thought. But what he said was, "That's claptrap, sir. There are already several thousand slaves in Texas today and with most of us coming from places like Virginia or South

Carolina, how do you figure that I'm going to stop you from bringing your slaves with you?"

Will waited for Maverick to respond, while thinking he had just summed up the biggest challenge as well as the best opportunity for changing the trajectory of Texas. He just needed to figure out how to get more northerners and Europeans to immigrate. The sandy-haired man glared back at him and replied, "Well, don't think that we're not going to be keeping an eye on you, Colonel Travis. If you try destroying our institutions, there'll be hell to pay." Without waiting for Will to respond, Maverick turned on his heels and stormed out of the cantina.

Will couldn't help but see Joe wore a fearful expression on his face. He leaned over and patted the former slave on the shoulder, "Don't worry Joe. Until you figure out what you want to do, you've got a job with me, if you want it."

As they walked out the cantina to return to the office of the *Sindico Procurador*, Joe replied, "Thank you, Mister William. Maybe for the time being, I'll be your servant, then."

Later, Will read the document formalizing Joe's freedom with a grin that split his face from ear to ear.

Manuel Martinez
To
Joe Travis
Republic of Texas
Ayuntamiento San Antonio de Bexar

Be it known to all men by these present that I, Manuel Martinez, of the Ayuntamiento of San Antonio de Bexar, Republic of Texas, acting under the authority of Alcalde Francisco Ruiz of Bexar, holding his position at the authority of the Provisional Government of the Republic of Texas, acting for and on behalf of William Barrett Travis, Colonel, have this day liberated and set free and fully and effectually manumitted, Joe Travis. Heretofore a slave for life, the lawful property of the said Colonel William Travis. The description of said Joe Travis being as follows to wit: About twenty-two years old, Five feet ten inches, very black and of good countenance. The said Joe Travis to enjoy and possess now and from henceforth the full exercise of all rights, benefits and privileges of a free man of color, free of any and all claim of servitude, slavery or services of the said William Barrett Travis, his heirs, Executors, and assignees and all other persons claiming or to claim forever.

In Testimony of this seal of Manumission, I have this day signed my name and affixed my seal this 25th day of March 1836.

Manuel Martinez

Sindico Procurador for the Ayuntamiento San Antonio de Bexar, Republic of Texas

Chapter 16

We, the people of the Republic of Texas, in order to form a government, establish justice, ensure domestic tranquility, provide for the common defence and general welfare, and to secure the blessings of liberty to ourselves and our posterity, in gratitude to our creator, do ordain and establish this constitution.

The nave of the church of San Fernando's adobe plastered walls had been recently painted. Sunlight streamed in from several windows, covering the walls and floors with warm, natural light. Will looked around the nave of the church, the pews now pushed to the side, replaced by a dozen large tables. Over sixty men were assembled in the church. Will sat at a table with Crockett, Seguin, Lorenzo de Zavala, and Jose Navarro. Earlier in the week, before the constitutional convention's start, the men of the army had protested they were being excluded from the convention. David Burnet and Sam Houston agreed and the result was Will, Crockett, and Seguin were now seated as delegates, elected by the soldiers at the Alamo.

Sam Houston strode through the double doors of the church, as he passed by their table, he nodded to Crockett and sat at the table to their right. Houston set his hat on the table. It was black and wide-brimmed and folded up to give the appearance of a tri-corner. Houston wore a gray suit jacket over a black vest. As he settled himself in his chair, a couple other men, seeing his arrival, joined him at the table.

Will suspected everything he knew about the Texas Revolution and its subsequent history was useless now. They were in uncharted waters. From his recollection of history, the constitution had been a hurried and rushed document, drafted in the weeks immediately following the March 2nd declaration of independence. But in his new reality, when word of Santa Anna's surrender reached Washington-on-the-Brazos, the entirety of the Texas provisional government suspended the session and hurried toward San Antonio, eager to put their imprint on any peace treaty with Santa Anna.

After the last few stragglers entered the church and took their seats, acting President Burnet stood and gaveled the convention into session. The sound of the gavel was still echoing off the adobe walls when there was a disturbance at the rear of the church. As his shadow crossed the threshold, an elderly Indian came through the door. Will noticed that the old man was garbed in plain brown woolen pants, soft doe-skinned moccasins, a calico shirt, and a vest that would make the biblical Joseph jealous for its brilliant hues. He wore a battered, black top hat which he removed as he took a seat next to Houston.

Burnet stood behind a small table which served purpose as a podium. He wore a perplexed look on his face, as the gavel, still in his hand, stayed fixed in the air, unmoving. "What's the meaning of this intrusion, General Houston?"

Houston patted the shoulder of the ancient Indian as he stood. He gave a slight bow to Burnet, "President Burnet, with your permission?" Burnet nodded slightly, a look of uncertainty on his face. "As you are aware, the provisional government in January empowered me to treat with the Cherokee tribe here in Texas. As of yet, no treaty has been ratified. Chief Bowles has come here both as a resident of Texas and as one of the elders of his people, to represent their interests."

Burnet finally set the gavel down and found his voice, "General Houston, I'm sure that you recognize that this is highly irregular. The Cherokee do not have legal standing here." Will thought Burnet was choosing his words with care as the interim President's eyes slid to a table where several prominent men from the American south sat. Several of them stood and applauded Burnet and shouted their agreement.

Equally revealing, Will thought, were those who didn't question the right of the old Cherokee to be seated. James Grant remained in his chair as did all the Tejanos who were present. Crockett leaned over and whispered in Will's ear, "Looks like Sam might could use a favor right about now."

When Burnet saw Crockett stand, he saw an opportunity to move the meeting along. He waved to those standing and said, "The convention will come to order. General Houston, if you'll please take your seat, the chair recognizes the former Congressman David Crockett, late of Tennessee."

Crockett nodded to Houston then acknowledged the men who had been standing up, with a half bow from his waist. "My fellow Americans." He paused for a moment, "No. That stopped being true when most of you fixed your signature on our declaration of independence more than a month ago. Every man, woman and child drawing breath in the land bound by the Rio Grande, the Sabine, and Red Rivers and by the Gulf of Mexico now lives under the banner of the Republic of Texas. So, if you'll allow me, my fellow delegates, to start over." He paused theatrically for a moment, "My fellow Texians, I applaud General Houston, for agreeing to serve our noble cause as General in our direst hour of need, even though the war was won on the banks of the Nueces River, I salute the General's commitment to Texas. Who here will stand with me and acknowledge that General Houston's love and fidelity to Texas knows no bounds."

For a moment, Will was spellbound by Crockett's deft mastery of the crowd, as he and the other men at the table stood and applauded Houston. He had adroitly reminded everyone present that it wasn't Houston who had won victory but that he was still doing his duty to Texas. Throughout the church, other men stood and applauded until every man was on his feet acknowledging Houston's service.

As the applause ended and the men sat, everyone directed their undivided attention back to Crockett. "As you know," he continued, "I was never one to shirk my duty neither during the late war with England nor during the wars with their Indian allies. But I trust that each of you remember, I have fought the long fight against Andy Jackson when he forced through Congress the Indian Removal Act. It was that fight that cost me my seat in Washington, if you recall. Now, as we discuss the constitution that we want to govern our lives and our nation, we have it in our power to do something extraordinary, in our new home and our new nation, the Republic of Texas. I ask each of you, whether you came here from New Jersey," he nodded his head toward Burnet, "or were born under the flag of Saint Andrew," he waved his hand to the table where James Grant sat, "or if you hail from Tennessee, or were born in South Carolina, like our brave and heroic Colonel Travis, here. We have been granted an opportunity by Almighty God above, to build something uniquely Texian here. I stand before you all now and ask that you join me and General Houston by welcoming the esteemed Chief Bowles of the Cherokee as an observer."

Before Crockett could sit, Will leapt to his feet and cried out, "I second the honorable Congressman Crockett, that this body permits Chief Bowles to sit as an observer upon this assembly."

Burnet, sensing an opportunity to take control of proceedings again, grabbed his gavel and hammered it on the table, "The motion has been seconded. All in favor of allowing Chief Bowles of the Cherokee to sit as an observer, say Aye." A clear majority of the room responded with a resounded "Aye". Burnet concluded, "The Ayes carry the motion. Chief Bowles shall be permitted to observe the convention."

Over the first few days of the convention, Will watched men like Crockett, Houston, and Zavala work with the other delegates to build consensus on issues. Burnet, Will thought, had allowed the convention to start on topics which were less controversial. Even so, after Samuel Carson, from North Carolina had outlined a provision to limit congressional terms to one year, Will posed a question during the debate, "If our representatives were to stand for election yearly, wouldn't that create a perpetual state of campaigning and electioneering?"

Will was amused as support for Carson's proposal withered after that. Despite a clear interest by several delegates to introduce short terms for office holders, in the end, they voted to match the US system for both the House of Representatives and the Senate. More importantly, Will thought, they had agreed to a single six-year term for the office of President and Vice President.

Another debate Will found interesting occurred after James Power, originally from Ireland, introduced a provision for proportional representation in the house of representatives. At one point, Powers addressed the delegates, "One of the functions of governance is to allow all voices to be heard, and a proportional allocation of representatives would allow like-minded men with minority views to have representation, without the need to be geographically concentrated."

Others offered arguments in favor and in opposition. As the debate wore on, Crockett rose and addressed the delegates, "My fellow Texians, I applaud Mr. Power and acknowledge the lack of representation his homeland endures at the hands of English politicians and it lends credence to his position. However, I believe that it is more laudable that each and every member of congress be held accountable to his constituents directly. While I admire Mr. Power, this proposal of his removes our ability to hold individuals accountable to their constituents, rendering an all or nothing proposition at the time of a general election. How would you go to your representative for redress?"

While several more delegates spoke on the issue, Will thought Crockett's argument sealed Power's proposal. The resulting vote by the delegates was predictable. While the Tejano and European delegates strongly favored the amendment, Crockett's view carried the day among the majority of American-born delegates.

The convention was in progress for more than a week, when Robert Potter, a North Carolinian, stood and upon recognition from Burnet, said, "My fellow Texians and delegates, I bring before you, for your consideration, a general provision to the constitution that will safeguard our rights." He paused as he looked over at Will's table, before reading, "No slave owner shall emancipate his slaves, without the consent of congress, unless he first send the slaves outside the limits of the republic. Nor shall any free person of African descent be permitted to live within the boundaries of the republic without the express consent of congress."

Incensed, Will leapt to his feet, and cried out, "What are you getting at Potter? Texas is for whites only? Negroes, Indians, and Mexicans not allowed? Who's your next target? The Irish?"

Potter shot back, "Don't put words in my mouth, Colonel Travis. I said no such thing."

Will looked over at Zavala and could tell that his words had struck home. But Potter continued, "I have no interest in Texas turning into New York, where freed darkies are allowed to come and go at their leisure." Potter sneered at Will as he sat. There was a muttering of support from the tables where the Southerners sat.

Will scarcely contained his rage, "So, you and me, we

can buy or sell a negro, but as soon as I decide to free him you'd hobble me with regulations? You hate it when the Yankees tell you how and under what circumstances you can sell your cotton or when they try to pass a tariff, but when it suits your fancy, you're quite willing to do the same thing when it comes to someone else's slaves. What's next? Stripping Texians of Mexican descent of their rights?"

Potter jeered at Will, "Pretty words from a newborn abolitionist."

Will jabbed his finger in the Southerner's direction, "Potter, I have earned the right to change my views when I helped to protect you and your rights on the Rio Grande and the Nueces. What the hell have you done for Texas? You lounge about and reap the reward that others have earned, growing fat and lazy on other men's labor."

Will was beyond any sense of caring and was ready to beat the other man into a bloody pulp when Potter hurried around the end of his table and, standing in the middle of the nave, cried, "You insult me, you yellow pup. If it weren't for Colonel Crockett, Santa Anna would be dancing on your grave!"

Will slid across the table and took two steps toward Potter, swinging his fist at the other man's nose. Potter's head snapped back as he fell against a table, blood running from his nose. As the president of the convention, Burnet allowed things to go too far; he pounded his gavel on the table, shouting. "Order!"

Potter turned toward the other Southerners, a look of triumph shining in his eyes. "I have been insulted and struck. I demand satisfaction!"

President Burnet repeatedly slammed the gavel, "Order! Sir, Order! Potter you're out of order. And

Colonel Travis, striking another delegate! You're out of order and sit, before I find you in contempt of the convention!"

Realizing his temper had gotten the better of him, Will immediately returned to his seat beside Crockett and in a low voice asked, "David, What I have done?"

Crockett shook his head, "Buck, if you're going to hit someone, hit 'em hard enough they go down and don't get back up. Bob Potter has gone and challenged you to a duel."

Will gulped. This wasn't how he imagined the day going. He knew better than to let his temper get the better of him. "How do I get out of this?"

"If you're of a mind to do so, go apologize for striking him."

Will began to stand, only to have Crockett push him back into his seat. "I said, if you're of a mind to do so, Buck. But before you go and do that, you need to think through what happens next if you do. First, your standing in the convention will suffer. Oh, I know it ain't right, and it may not make a lick of sense, but most of these Southern boys, they'd rather tar and feather you as an abolitionist than as a coward, and I'm afraid if you apologize, it will damage your reputation. It could even cost you your position in the army, so before you get in a mind to go apologize, consider the cost."

Will swore under his breath and replied in a voice as low as Crockett's, "Will you be my second, David?" It struck him as entirely too bizarre, to risk permanent disfigurement or death over a perceived slight of honor. *"But I did nearly manage to break his nose."* Will thought with momentary satisfaction.

On each table in the Church's nave, there was a small stack of paper. Will took a sheet, and inked a pen and hurriedly wrote across the paper, *"Accepted. As the challenged, by rights I choose the saber as the weapons."*

He quickly folded the sheet and gave it to David. "If I recall correctly, as my second, you'll arrange the details?"

Crockett opened the letter and read Will's note. He raised his eyebrows when he reached the line about sabers. He closed the letter and leaned in. "I'll give him the note. But what the hell are you thinking about Sabers. He may insist on pistols. I know, he challenged you and by rights, it's your prerogative to choose weapons, but most of our august body would view it favorably if he requests pistols for you to agree."

Will shrugged in response. It wasn't what he wanted to hear. He had taken a semester of fencing in college, and fancied himself halfway competent back in the day. But since finding himself in Travis' body, he found a certain enjoyment practicing sword drills with Juan Seguin, and he felt confident between the techniques learned in college and the recent practice he had an advantage over Potter.

Crockett rose from his chair and ambled over to Potter's table where he leaned in and in a whisper traded words with the hot-tempered North Carolinian. A moment later he handed the note to William Menefee, originally of Tennessee, who Potter had chosen as his second.

After Crockett returned to his seat, Will eyed the two men at the table, as Menefee opened the note. He raised his eyebrows as he arrived at the note's end. He handed the note to Potter, who read it. When he read Will's weapon selection he raised his head and looked over to Will with a perplexed look. Will smiled, baring his teeth, daring the man to question his choice of weapons.

The matter temporarily settled, the many eyes which switched from watching Potter one moment to Will another, eventually focusing their attention back on the current debate, as though there was nothing more interesting than discussing the ways and means by which a slave owner could free his property. At one point, the parish priest came in and lit the lamps along the walls, at twilight. As the evening grew late, and consensus proved elusive, Menefee, as Potter's second passed a note to Crockett, who read it and handed it to Will.

Let the matter be settled tomorrow morning at nine sharp. Should I win, you withdraw your opposition. Should you win, I will drop my petition. Robert Potter

Will nodded, and Potter stood and upon recognition by Burnet, said, "Let us end our debate tonight regarding my proposal, and reconvene tomorrow at noon, where a vote shall be taken."

Will seconded the motion. Given the recalcitrance by the Southerners throughout the evening's debate, Will worried the only option left to him was to kill Potter.

The sun was well into a cloudless sky when a few minutes before nine, Will and Crockett walked out of the Alamo gate, heading toward the site Crockett and Menefee had selected the previous night. The duel would take place a few hundred yards west of the fort on the east bank of the San Antonio River.

A footbridge lay across the acequia running along the western wall. Scrub brush and plants grew along the narrow banks, and the scent of honeysuckle was heavy in the April air as the two men walked through knee-high green grass. Will breathed in deeply, thinking this was simply too good a day to die.

James Grant, serving in his capacity as surgeon, was already in place, a long trundle table set up next to where he stood. In the distance, Will could see Potter and Menefee riding over the bridge across the San Antonio River. Both parties arrived on the field of honor at the same time. Will desperately wanted to tell Potter this was simply a misunderstanding. He wasn't afraid to fight. Will's entire adult life proved that, but a duel seemed stupid. Crockett had reminded him he wasn't simply fighting to determine the rights to free one's slave but also to avoid any taint of cowardice.

Will knew his heart, and the fear he felt, while not the voice of an old friend, was one he had grown use to long before he displaced Travis. He'd learned to live with fear in the desert sands of Iraq. Crockett and Menefee approached the table and examined the sabers. To avoid giving Will an apparent advantage, Will's own saber remained in his office. The two weapons had been provided by Erasmo Seguin.

Will looked back at the wall of the Alamo and saw Juan Seguin standing atop the wall, along with several hundred other soldiers, watching as rules for the duel were settled between the two men's seconds. It was too late to order them to their duties. He realized it wouldn't matter anyway, as the eastern bank of the river was lined with people from town, who came to watch.

While he tried to clear his mind and focus on the task at hand, Will overheard Crockett talking with Menefee at the weapons table. "Bill, are you sure your man won't consider retracting the challenge?"

Menefee shook his head, "Not going to happen, David. Bob's mighty riled. Your man shouldn't have struck him. It was intemperate. Bob demands satisfaction. Until one or the other is unable to continue."

Crockett pursed his lips and nodded, returning to Will's side. "I guess you heard it all?"

With an economy of motion, Will nodded once. "Let's do it."

Crockett placed his hand on Will's chest. "Just one second, Buck. I got a feeling Bob's not interested just drawing blood, I suspect he'll try to kill you."

Will barked a harsh laugh. "That'll make two of us, then."

Silk sashes had been laid across the ground where Will and Potter stood ten feet apart. Will held the saber in his hand. Its balance was very similar to his. He observed his opponent and saw Potter held the saber correctly in his right hand.

Menefee spoke quietly, but in the still morning it echoed in Will's ear like a gunshot. "Begin!"

The two duelers stepped across their lines at the same time. Will held his weapon at the ready, advancing on Potter. With less polish, his opponent sprang forward, blade outstretched. With his right side facing Will, Potter shuffled his feet forward, rapidly closing the distance. Will twisted his saber, parrying. He stepped to his right, as Potter continued forward.

As Potter turned around, Will lunged, attempting to skewer him. Potter backpedaled. The tip of the blade grazed his vest with no visible result. Retreating a step, Will returned to his en garde position. Potter fingered the vest where he found a tiny rip. His face grew florid and he pursued Will across the grass, swinging the saber in tightly controlled arcs. Will retreated, parrying each swipe, watching his opponent's eyes as they blazed in anger, looking for his opportunity.

Having fallen back a dozen paces, Will twirled to his left, swatting Potter's weapon aside. He sank back into his defensive position, waiting to see Potter's next move. The other man whirled around, and stormed toward him. Rather than retreat, Will brought his saber up, as the blades clanged together, and he pressed forward, pushing Potter's blade back. Potter's face, distorted with rage was only inches away. Will ground out, "Yield!"

Potter tried forcing the blade away and spat back, "Never, you damned nigger lover!"

Enough was enough, Will thought, as he pushed forward with his blade, forcing Potter to step back. Potter attempted to parry the coming lunge, only to find Will had feinted. Turning his lunge into a powerful slash, his blade slammed into Potter's just above the pommel. The saber sailed out of Potter's stunned fingers, landing in a patch of lush, green grass.

While his opponent registered the loss of his saber, Will nicked Potter's arm, drawing blood. Disarmed and bleeding, Potter's eyes blazed in anger for a moment, as he stared into Will's eyes. With a subtle glance towards his second, Potter diverted his eyes and placed his hand over his injured arm and quietly said, "I yield."

Will wanted to hate Potter, as his opponent stood on the field, disarmed, holding his right hand over a cut on his left arm, where blood oozed through his fingers, dripping to the ground. But the other man, now composed, returned his stare, unflinching. Gritting his teeth, the other man said, "You have bested me,

Colonel Travis. For now. As agreed, I will withdraw my petition."

Will smiled widely, as he heard cheering coming from the walls of the Alamo. His soldiers lustily shouted his name, "Travis! Travis!"

The Bexarenos on the east bank of the river were also cheering. It appeared that everyone loves a winner. As Will laid the weapon back on the table, Crockett patted him on the back and said, "Nicely done, Buck."

Will grinned. "Are you going to remind me I'm mortal, David?"

Chuckling, Crockett shook his head. "Lordy, I hope you don't need me to remind you of that. But I would suggest you get used to having enemies. You won today, but Potter's not going anywhere. Today it was swords, but look to your safety, Buck. Who knows what he'll bring next time."

When the convention reconvened in the afternoon, following lunch, Robert Potter, with his left arm wrapped and in a sling, withdrew his petition. But if Will had hoped that the day would take the deliberations in a more amiable direction, he was wrong.

Thomas Rusk stood and upon recognition by President Burnet, said, "In an effort to provide an orderly set of provisions by which citizenship shall be conferred, I would like to enter into record the attached general provision." He walked up to Burnet's table and gave him the proposed provision.

Rusk returned to his table and read it aloud, "All persons, excepting Africans, the descendants of Africans, and Indians, who were residing in Texas on the day of the declaration of independence shall be considered citizens of the republic and entitled to all the privileges of such. All citizens now living in Texas who have not received their portion of land in like manner as colonists shall be entitled to their land in the following proportion and manner: Every head of a family shall be entitled to one league and labor of land; and every single man of the age of seventeen and upward shall be entitled to the third part of one league of land. All citizens who may have, previously to the adoption of this constitution, received their league of land as heads of families, and their quarter of a league as single persons, shall receive such additional quantity as will make the quantity of land received by them equal to one league and labor, and one-third of a league, unless by bargain, sale, or exchange they have transferred, or may henceforth transfer, their right to said land, or a portion thereof, to some other citizen of the republic; and in such case, the person to whom such right shall have been transferred shall be entitled to the same as fully and amply as the persons asking the transfer might or could have been. No alien shall hold land in Texas except by titles emanating directly from the government of this republic. But if any citizen of this republic should die intestate or otherwise his children or heirs shall inherit his estate, and aliens shall have a reasonable time to take possession of and dispose of the same, in a manner hereafter to be pointed out by law. Orphan children whose parents were entitled to land under the colonization laws of Mexico and who now reside in the republic shall be entitled to all the rights of which their parents were possessed at the time of their death. The citizens of the republic shall not be compelled to reside on the land, but shall have their lines plainly marked."

Will felt a heavy hand resting on his shoulder and turned and saw Crockett, wearing a deep frown, shaking his head slightly at him. After the intensity of the previous day, Will was inclined to heed Crockett's unspoken advice, for the time being. Will then saw Sam Houston, who was standing next to his friend, Chief Bowles, wearing a stormy expression. Once Burnet acknowledged him, he said, "I move that the word 'Indians' be stricken from the provision."

The room erupted into turmoil as several of Rusk's allies booed Houston. President Burnet, clearly frustrated, gaveled the delegates to silence. Bowing slightly to Burnet, Houston continued, "I allow that, at the moment, a state of war exists between us and the Comanche, but no such conflict exists between us and our Cherokee neighbors. We have been given an opportunity by a merciful Providence to do the right thing and correct one of the few things that Andy Jackson got wrong."

While there were glares from some of the men sitting amid the bloc of Southern-born delegates, there were many thoughtful faces around the room. Houston continued, "Not only should we grant them their land in the treaty recently negotiated, but we should extend citizenship to those in the civilized tribes, like the Cherokee, who swear allegiance to the ideals of the Republic and our constitution."

Several men rose in quick succession, speaking both for and against Houston's amendment to Rusk's provision. An idea sparked into Will's mind and he stood as the last speaker finished. Burnet looked at him and said, "Colonel, you're not going to incite any more violence this afternoon, I hope." Will wasn't certain how to take it, until he saw a glimmer of a smile on Burnet's normally dour face.

Will smiled wryly and replied, "No, Mr. President." As he weighed his words, he had always thought the reservations were a terrible injustice, wondering what the US might have looked like had the country been willing to integrate the American Indians into the melting pot which he thought defined the country. "My fellow Texians, I agree with General Houston that any member of the civilized tribes, like the Cherokee, who reside in Texas should have citizenship bestowed upon them, upon meeting the requirements he proposed. I differ with him in one respect. Our American tradition rightly has always prized the right of any man to own his own homestead. It is a cardinal principal of common law we hold dear. While I would happily yield my understanding to Chief Bowles, as I understand it, the Cherokee have a somewhat different appreciation of land ownership. I believe that view, when it has come into conflict with ours, has invariably left the Cherokees as the beggars in the relationship. Rather than deeding land to the tribe, by treaty, I propose that any Cherokee brave currently living in Texas today, be allocated six hundred forty acres of land in the area wherein they currently reside, deeded to them individually, just as legally binding as the deeds to our own lands." Will stopped there, figuring that the other delegates didn't need to hear his melting pot theories.

Like the previous day, this session ran late into the evening. More amendments to the original provision were proposed and most of the delegates spoke for or against the various amendments. When the convention voted on the proposal, they voted that Indians would be allowed citizenship if their tribe agreed to individual ownership of property, and if the tribes divested any communal ownership to the individual members.

Also removed from the original provision was the term, "descendants of Africans." A clear majority of the delegates adamantly insisted the constitution include no language restricting the ownership of slaves. But, apart from a plurality of delegates from the American South, there was no consensus on what percentage of blood made one of African descent. On that issue, the only consensus the delegates found was leaving that for a future congress to decide.

Chapter 17

Winter died with a whimper, and spring seemed to be on life support, Will thought as he sat in the same chair, at the same table as he had for the better part of three weeks. The nave of the church was muggy and warm as the mid-April afternoon waned. Will's tenure in the convention, he knew, had been filled with contention as he worked to mitigate the worst excesses of his fellow Southerners. As he stood, he felt like he had a large target affixed to his chest as President Burnet recognized him, "My fellow delegates, I would like to submit the following general provision for consideration." Will took a loose piece of paper and placed it in front of Burnet, as dozens of men had done over the preceding weeks.

Holding a second copy, Will returned to his seat and read the provision, "Congress retains the right to regulate slavery within the entirety of the republic and impose such limits as it may deem necessary regarding the importation of slaves from the United States, and reserves the right, enumerated in Section II Article I to assess a tariff on such imports, as it deems necessary to support the general funds of the Republic of Texas."

As Will settled into his chair, James Collinsworth, a delegate representing the Brazoria area, but originally from Tennessee, stood and after being recognized by Burnet, spoke, "Colonel Travis, may I ask why you would put into the hands of congress this burden? Many of us have travelled from across Texas, putting our lives and property at risk, first at Washington-on-the-Brazos to sign the declaration of independence and now here in Bexar where we endeavor to lay the constitutional grounds of our Republic. Many of us, formerly of the Southern states, brought our property with us. And others came here for new opportunities that would provide them the chance to amass such wealth as lies within their God-given abilities to generate. I feel it is entirely proper to remove this burden from the future congress so that they can govern our fair land without the burden of slavery being a constant divider. You have fought us on giving every white immigrant free land, successfully, I might add. Now you fight to limit our right to bring our slaves with us as we encourage our former neighbors back home to join us in our new nation. As Congressman Crockett reminded us earlier, you're tender in your years, and lack the experience that many of your fellow delegates have. At every step of the way, you seemed determined to force us to relitigate the status of our peculiar institution. Why, sir?"

Collinsworth remained standing, staring at him, as the room waited in expectation for Will's response. He was certainly more eloquent than Potter had been, and to give him his due, as a slave owner, Collinsworth had asked a relevant question. As Will stood, he looked around the room, gauging the mood of the delegates.

Apart from laughing at Collinsworth's wit, Crockett now nodded encouragingly at Will. Zavala and the Tejanos, as well as those delegates from Europe silently waited for Will's response.

"Mr. Collinsworth, I commend you for your service and readily concede that absent your effort, along with the other delegates, that there would have been no declaration of independence. For your service, James, I applaud you." Will directed his applause to Collinsworth and watched others as they responded with polite applause.

As the men in the church grew silent, Will continued, "I must concede that while my much esteemed colleague, Congressman Davy Crockett was riding lightning bolts across the Mississippi, I was still in short pants. Measured against his exploits, I concede that I am wet behind the ears. Of course, if one were to believe all of the exploits published about my friend, Davy, one might be inclined to think that in comparison, Methuselah of the Old Testament, might also be considered wet behind the ears."

Most of the delegates laughed, but Crockett's guffaw was the loudest. Will continued when the laughter died, "But were it not for our mutual efforts earlier this year, the declaration of independence may have been for naught."

Collinsworth conceded the point with a slight bow., as Will continued, "After watching the debacle back east between the land of my birth, South Carolina and Andy Jackson over the abominable tariffs, I think it showcases the need within our own constitution to provide our legislators the widest latitude possible within a constitution to make and change laws. The right to regulate slavery and taxation are simply two tools that will allow our congress to function to the fullest extent possible. But several of my colleagues here have opposed efforts that I and others have introduced so that our Republic can pay its bills. When I urged we limit new free grants of land to only those who served in the republic's army and navy, many of you fought this and wanted to give away our public lands to any Johnny-come-lately. Our first obligation is to our Republic and its common defense, but we cannot continually expect to defend ourselves from the threat that Mexico will continue to pose to our south, or stop the Indians from raiding out of the Comancheria if we have no money to pay for it. I find it ironic, Mr. Collingsworth that you had no objections to taxing the labor and products of the shipmaster who bring in the cargoes that are the lifeblood of trade into Texas. But when I propose simply leaving the door open to a similar tax on slaves that represent your wealth, and that allow you to stand, economically above your fellow Texians, many of whom toil away in poverty providing for their wives and children, you protest. Why do you begrudge them the benefits of the protection that such tax revenue would provide?"

Unwilling to wait for Burnet to recognize him, Collinsworth, shot back at Will, "I believe, Colonel Travis, that you are simply wrapping up your abolitionism in a pretty little bow. What has become of you, man? Since you and Crockett captured Santa Anna, you have gone soft and freed your own negro, and now, you seem hell-bent on retarding the advancement of our economic interests."

Will tensed up, ready with a sharp retort to Collinsworth's harsh words, when Crockett placed a restraining hand on his shoulder. President Burnet slammed the gavel on the table and growled, "One more outburst like that James, and I'll find you in contempt of the convention, sir." He swept his hand that was holding the gavel around the room and said, "Fellow delegates, I have had all of the failure to follow decorum as I am willing to tolerate. You don't speak until the chair recognizes you!" Collinsworth shot a nasty glare encompassing both Burnet and Will.

The debate was winding down as the day wore on, and Will feared that the mood of the room indicated his proposed provision was headed for defeat. Just as Burnet was set to close debate, Crockett stood, as though from sleeping in his chair, and said, "President Burnet, before debate is closed, may I have a moment to speak on the proposal?"

With a nod from Burnet, Crocket continued, "I have long made my views for support of the common, western farmer known. And frequently have been keen to avoid taxing unduly the people that I have represented. In a country of thirteen million, it was easy to do. But I fear if we take away the tools of state, that we may fail to protect our farmers who rightly fear attack at the hands of the Comanche. If there was no doubt that we could protect and defend our borders with a citizen militia, I might agree with Mr. Collinsworth, that a property tax is unnecessary. However, I do not believe we can adequately protect our people or our borders without a strong army and navy. It hurts me at my core to say this, but our constitution should give us every tool available to provide for our common defense, up to and including property taxes and land taxes. How can we say no to our future and our shared need for defense by voting against Colonel Travis' provision?"

As Crockett returned to his seat, Will looked across the nave at Collinsworth's table, where the five men sitting around it had an air of defeat. When Burnet called the question and tallied the vote, every delegate who was born outside of the American South voted for its passage. Even among the Southern delegates, nearly a third of the delegates crossed over and voted for the provision. The proposal to allow taxation on the import of slaves as well as a property tax passed by a slim margin.

By the time the convention adjourned for the night, normally nearly all the three thousand souls making San Antonio home in April of 1836 were typically asleep. But between Houston's soldiers and the more than five dozen delegates, cantinas and saloons were doing brisk business well past midnight. Will found himself with Crockett and Lorenzo de Zavala sitting at a table in one of the cantinas bustling with business.

As a pretty senorita brought out a large platter piled high with tamales and a large bowl of baked beans to their table, Will observed Zavala. The fair-skinned Mexican was a couple of years younger than Crockett's forty-nine years, and he wore his thick, deep-brown hair slicked back. Turning his attention to his food, Will unwrapped a couple of tamales as Zavala said, "As you know, I'm no more native to Texas than you or David, here. Had that fool of a dictator not destroyed our federal system, I would likely have returned to Mexico City, where I imagine I would have dabbled in politics. But, I want you to know, Colonel, that what you did this evening was brave."

Will blushed at Zavala's compliment, until he continued, "Brave, yes. But you're too much like a young priest straight from the seminary. You have fire and determination, but you have too little of the diplomat in you."

Will swallowed a bite of the tamales, the chicken tasting bland, as Zavala's critique hit home.

Crockett nodded and said, "I don't like hitting a man when he's down, Buck, but you remind me of a neighbor I once had back in Western Tennessee. In our younger days, the two of us knew how to cut loose back when we were younger. And I hate to admit it, but he brewed a better moonshine than any I'd managed. One day, he got himself religion. It ain't that he gave up drinking swearing and dancing, but he took to railing against every vice all the time. Every fight was the good fight to him and he lost most of his friends along the way. You already know that I got no truck with Negros one way or t'other, and as God is my witness, I've worked beside a few in my younger days. But, I truly think the better of you for freeing your man, Joe. You showed yourself to be a man of character. But the point I'm making, like Lorenzo, is you need to pick your battles with men like Potter and Collinsworth. Hell, boy, I like you, and I want to keep liking you, and if some two-legged polecat winds up sticking his pig-sticker into you, I'd be mighty sorry."

As the three men finished their meal, Zavala said, "I would hate for you to think that all David and I are offering you is critique, William. I have grown fond of you. And like you, I abhor the scourge that is slavery. When Mexico held her own constitutional convention in 1824, I was there and watched as we outlawed slavery throughout all of Mexico. It was a constant thorn in my side to watch my American neighbors flaunting our anti-slavery laws by claiming their slaves were simply indentured servants. I don't presume to put words in David's mouth, not when he so eloquently does it himself, but we can see where the winds of this convention are blowing and I believe you have done much to limit the worst excesses of men like Potter and Collinsworth and their effort to favor slavery in our own system." Will noticed Crockett was nodding his agreement with Zavala.

"Further," Zavala said, "you forced them to allow Indians like the Cherokee to become citizens and stopped them from treating someone who is only one-part Negro no better than a slave. And you kept them from driving men like your Joe out of the republic. They intended to lock slavery firmly into the constitution then make the process for amending it so cumbersome as to lock future generations of Texians into a document that would have to be torn apart to change it. Because of you, they failed and now Congress will regulate it and tax it and if later they want to change it, you made that possible. You kept them from giving the best of our public lands to more slave owners. Equally as important, you set the stage for making sure that our government will have the resources needed to fight our next battle."

Will was furiously blushing once Zavala finished. Seeing Will's discomfort, he said, "Everything I said is true, but equally true is that you've made some powerful enemies, William. Please watch your back."

As they settled their tab with the pretty senorita, Zavala and Crockett bade Will a good night. Before returning to the room he had rented in town the Tennessean said, "Buck, you're a better man than I was at your age. I admire that you stick by your convictions. I am proud to know you, so please, let me repeat what Lorenzo said, and keep an eye on your backside."

The brass bell hanging in the church tower struck one o'clock before Will and his companions departed from the cantina. As the owner of the cantina was dousing candles, a couple of delegates originally from Ohio and England congratulated him for his stand during the convention. A couple of Southern delegates in the cantina simply glared at him from their tables.

He untied his horse from the cantina's hitching post and nudged it onto Alameda Street, following the road toward the river. As he let the animal set its own pace, Will thought, "David and Lorenzo are right. I believe things are going to be a lot better than those fools did in the history I remember, and now the pro-slavery faction has been weakened." He sighed, as he thought back to the moment when he realized that there were nowhere near enough votes to make slavery outright illegal. It was only a week ago, when he sounded out Juan Seguin and James Grant and found neither of them would risk conflict over slavery. Both men told him that it was suicidal to directly threaten men like Potter. He shook his head as he thought about how entrenched the system was becoming, even in Texas, when a European like James Grant thought the risk of opposition too high.

As the shoes of his horse thudded across the wooden planks of the bridge, his spirits picked up as he reminded himself that he had driven a couple of nails into slavery's coffin. He hoped he would be around when the carcass of the atrocious institution was buried forever in Texas. From there, his thoughts drifted toward the apparent alliance growing between Crockett and Zavala, "I bet David will pick Lorenzo as his running mate, if he ever decides to actually throw his hat into the ring."

The moonlight gave Will a good look at the walls of the Alamo and he could see the gatehouse. James Neal, who had returned from his family emergency more than a month previous, was in the process of removing the lunette, which had blocked the gatehouse.

Along the side of the road, Will heard the knee-high grass swaying gently in the night breeze. As he turned onto the road leading to the fort's gate, he breathed in deeply, smelling the sweet fragrance of bluebonnets in bloom. Will felt a sharp sting slap the side of his head, as he heard a loud crack of a rifle shatter the still night air. Instinctively his left hand reached up to his head where he felt wet stickiness, above his ear. The loud boom reverberated across the still, dark prairie as his horse reared up on its hind legs. Holding on with one hand, Will felt the reins slip through his fingers, as he slid from the saddle. His body slowly slipping to the right, his right hand, no longer grasping the reins, brushed against the saddle sheath, where he kept his sword. His fingers snatched at the sword's hilt as he felt his body toppling to the right. Falling from the saddle, his fingers closed around the grip, only to have the sword slip from his grasp after clearing the scabbard. He landed hard on the side of the road, as the sword landed a few feet away. Although the fall took his breath away, Will stretched out his right hand grasping at dirt until his fingers found the cool metal of the pommel. He lay on the ground, gasping for air as he tried to fill his lungs.

When he tried sitting up, Will couldn't see anything out of his left eye, but he heard heavy footsteps racing toward him through the tall grass. With his left hand, he wiped away blood which smeared across his face but let him see a bit out of his left eye. He knew he needed to stand. Whoever was running toward him would arrive at any moment. Bile rose in his throat as he struggled to his knees. "*Please, God, don't let me throw up*," went through his mind.

The grass rustled right behind him as the footsteps slowed then stopped. A gravelly voice from behind said, "Well, looky here, I done bagged myself a goddamned nigger lover. Don't bother standing up. It won't do you no good."

He heard a rustling of clothes behind him then a clicking noise. In Will's mind, there was no doubt it was the sound of a pistol being cocked. The blood had run back into his left eye, from where the bullet had cut his scalp above his ear. As he clenched his fists, he realized his right hand still gripped the sword's hilt.

"You been warned and you done ignored real good advice, mister abolitionist. Now you're going to die!"

Will rolled to his right, as he heard the flint spark against the steel plate. Almost immediately the powder in the barrel ignited, propelling the lead ball forward at six hundred feet per second. Will heard it whistle as it came within a couple of inches of his left ear. As he fell to his right, he threw his left shoulder backward and brought the sword around, in an arc and saw the features of the would-be assassin come into focus in Will's one clear eye. He was a tall man, who, in the moonlight, appeared to have a black beard and long black hair. Will saw smoke curling out of the barrel, that the other man still held, pointing toward where Will's head had been a split second before, as the sword in Will's hand, pierced his stomach. A startled look replaced the angry expression, as a soft "oof" escaped his lips.

The weapon tumbled from the other man's hands, landing with a soft thud in the grass. The gun was followed a moment later by the man as his knees buckled and he collapsed, laying crumpled in the grass. As Will dizzily climbed to his feet, the sword's blade glistened in the moonlight, with a dark stain. The would-be assassin's breathing was labored and shallow.

Will's legs felt wobbly and he tried to stay on them as he heard several feet running toward him from the Alamo. With his one clear eye, he saw a couple of lanterns bobbing along, lighting the way ahead of the running men. The first to arrive was one of Seguin's cavalrymen, an experienced lieutenant by the name of Gregorio Esparza. In a startled voice he cried out, "*Dios mio*! Colonel, what in the hell happened here?" A couple more men, dressed in the gray jackets of the New Orleans Greys were hard on the lieutenant's heels.

Will attempted to focus his clear eye on the cavalry officer and replied, "I appear to have made an enemy." The sword slipped from Will's fingers and he felt himself sliding away, as the young officer appeared to retreat from him until the world went black.

Chapter 18

When he cracked opened his eyes, Will woke to see James Grant leaning over him, bandaging the side of his head. He croaked, "Have I died and gone to some hell reserved for Scottish adventurers?"

Grant chuckled, "'Tis good you're awake. From your speech, I'd say about half your wits are intact," smiling down at Will, he said, "your boys came and fetched me from town, said you needed a doctor. You took a nasty concussion when that bullet grazed your scalp. I'm wrapping it in boiled linen. Like most head wounds, you bled like a stuck pig. You may find over the next couple of days, you're subject to some nasty headaches, but overall, with a little rest, you'll be fine."

Will attempted to slide up in the bed, and noticed he was in the Alamo's hospital. The revelation fled from his mind as his head swam from a wave of nausea and dizziness that swept over him. Grant placed his hand on Will's shoulder, "Dinna be moving. A concussion is a nasty way to wake up."

As the queasiness settled, Will asked, "What of the man who tried to kill me, James, what happened to him?"

Grant shook his head, "A gut wound is a foul thing. He lingered on a few hours but died before sunup."

"Any idea who he was?" Will asked.

A shadow filled the window next to Will's cot, and he heard Juan Seguin's voice. "His name was Tom Roberts. He was with Bowie's volunteers up until a month ago. He was reported missing on our muster rolls around the time the government showed up last month."

Will closed his eyes, as another wave of nausea rolled over him. When it passed, he said, "Thanks, Juan. Anything else about him that I should know?"

A heavy bag of coins landed on the table beside him. "We found thirty Spanish silver dollars on him, but other than that, there was nothing to let us know who paid for his services."

Will laughed until the pain in his head caused him to grimace, "Thirty pieces of silver. Sweet Jesus, but that puts me in very fine company, wouldn't y'all agree?"

Seguin chuckled, "Well, after the past few weeks, Buck, I know a few men who would happily crucify you. I'd best get going, I don't want to be late getting to San Fernando for today's session. I'm sure the news has already arrived, but I will let everyone know that you'll make a speedy recovery."

"The hell you will, Juan," Will replied. "You're going to help me up and we'll go together. I'm not going to give those pompous jackasses, Potter or Collinsworth the satisfaction of thinking they've won this round."

Thirty minutes later, Will, head pounding and stomach churning, was riding into San Antonio, with Seguin by his side. Behind the two officers rode a troop of a dozen men from the Alamo. Seguin asked, "Do you believe any of the delegates were behind this?"

Will thought better of any head gestures, as the jarring gait of the horse sent shockwaves of pain into his head. He managed, "It is possible, but unlikely that the money came from directly from that lot. Think of what would happen to any delegate if the money led back to him."

Seguin pushed, "Don't you think that any of them had something to do with the attempt on your life?"

"I didn't say that, Juan. Only that evidence, if we could find any, would not likely point directly to them. But, if you have any luck finding a connection, certainly let me know. I'd love to see Potter in jail. No, I'd rather see him hanging from tree."

When they arrived at the church, the steely-eyed sergeant, in command of the horsemen, said with a lilting Irish accent, "Now, Colonel Travis, if you're needing anything, and I mean anything at all, you just let us know, we'll be in the plaza."

As he dismounted, Will turned to the sergeant and replied, "Thank you, but I trust that won't be necessary. But should any of you decide to kill me, I hope you'll hold out for more than thirty pieces of silver."

The sergeant, relaxing his vigilance for a moment, smiled warmly at Will and said, "Faith, Colonel, God bless you, sir, but I doubt you're worth a penny more than our Lord and Savior."

When they entered the church, Will and Seguin were mobbed by a crowd of the delegates, calling out and asking about the assassination attempt. Lorenzo de Zavala edged up to Will and took him by the elbow and led him over to their table, where Crockett was waiting, wearing a deep expression of concern on his face. He leaned over and placed his hand gently on Will's shoulder and quietly said, "Boy, you have no idea how glad I am to see that you're no worse for wear than you are. You had me plum worried sick when I heard about the attempt on your life."

Will smiled wanly and replied, "I feel much worse for wear, David. Like I was rode hard and put up wet."

An uncomfortable silence descended on the delegates, nearly every eye in the room fixed on Will. Burnet, as always, stood at the head table, his dour expression firmly planted on his face. Will thought he saw a look pass between him and Houston, at the next table. Will turned to look at Houston and noticed that as the General stood, he nodded at Crockett, like a co-conspirator. "President Burnet, if I may," Houston said, as he stood. With the permission of the chair, Houston walked around to stand in the middle of the nave, where he scanned the entire room, finally settling his glare at the table where Robert Potter and James Collinsworth sat.

"When our children and grandchildren study the history of our republic, and its foundational document, is there any man here that wants them to learn of the attempt last night on Colonel Travis' life?" He paused as he stared daggers at several of his fellow Southerners. Several delegates shifted in their chairs, looking anywhere but at Houston, while others cast inquisitive glances around, wondering who among them would be brazen enough to attempt to kill one of their members in the shadows of night. Houston resumed, "It is self-evident that our passions have been raised as we have deliberated how best to govern our new nation. While we must soldier on and do the good work our fellow Texians have sent us to do, much of the heaviest lifting is now behind us."

Many of Houston's fellow delegates settled back in

their chairs as he spoke, reminded as they were of how much they had already accomplished. He continued, "I have come to realize even once we have completed our responsibility here, that there is still much to be done and I would be remiss if I rested on the laurels of our present accomplishments. After consulting with President Burnet, I have decided once our work here is done, that I will return north with Chief Bowles and adjudicate their existing land claims, acting as an agent from the provisional government."

Crockett and several other men politely applauded as Houston returned to his chair. Burnet nodded at Houston and said, "Does anyone oppose, Sam Houston's appointment as commissioner to the civilized tribes in Texas, upon completion of our constitutional convention?"

While several men wore surly expressions, no one raised any objections, and Houston's appointment was unanimous.

President Burnet said, "Sam Houston's appointment as commissioner creates an urgent need for you, our delegates to act. Texas cannot afford to be without a commanding general for our army, yet, Sam's appointment leaves vacant his military office."

All the secretive looks between Burnet, Houston and Crockett started to fall into place in Will's pounding head. He was caught by surprise when James Grant stood and said, "As one who has served with Colonel William Barrett Travis, I would like to nominate him to the rank of Brigadier General, commander of all Texian forces, effective immediately."

Crockett stood and nodding at several others who were also now standing, said, "I would like to second Colonel Grant's motion. Having served with Colonel

Travis over the past couple of months, I can assure any other delegate that he will fulfill the responsibilities due the rank with utmost diligence and a keen ability."

Burnet nodded at Crockett, and with a sardonic smile directed toward several tablesful of Southerners, asked, "Are there any objections to Colonel Grant's motion?"

As Robert Potter started to stand, Collinsworth, who sat beside him, reached up and grabbed him by the shoulder and pulled him back into his seat. While Collinsworth whispered into his ear, Potter sagged under the words of his compatriot. When the tense moment passed, Collinsworth stood and said, "Given the heavy burden that the command of the army would place upon Colonel Travis, I will acquiesce to Mr. Crockett's wishes on the condition that Colonel Travis resign his duties to the convention, allowing him to focus on protecting our frontier from the depredations of Mexicans and Comanche alike."

Crockett held up a hand to the Southerner and said, "A moment, if you please." He leaned in to Will and said, "Buck, the big issues are settled. I've obtained agreements from several other delegates that all of the ground that you have won here at the convention will be protected. Those damn-fool jackanapes, parading as Southern gentlemen, will not be allowed to undo any of the provisions you and I have backed."

Will nodded his head slowly, as the migraine pounding like a jackhammer, continued its unrelenting attack. Quietly, he replied, "Thank you, David. I'm not sure what I think of your scheme, but please pass on my thanks to your fellow conspirators. I know that you'll keep Potter and his allies from getting too big for their britches. I agree, I will resign from the convention."

Immediately after the convention passed Crockett's resolution appointing Will as general, he slowly and painfully scrawled the name of William B. Travis, as he resigned from the convention and accepted command of the Texian army. During the time he had been in the church, one of the cavalrymen who had accompanied him and Seguin, found a wagon. As he exited the convention, he collapsed into the wagon bed. He lay in the back, eyes screwed shut against the bright April morning, as the wagon rolled back to the Alamo.

April 29th, 1836

To the honorable John Hall,

Commander of Ordnance of Harpers Ferry, Virginia

I am writing to inquire about the purchase of a quantity of your rifles, a certain number of your model 1833 Hall Carbines. I have been authorized by the provisional government of the Republic of Texas to purchase 500 of your excellent carbines, rifled to a .52 caliber at the price of $20 in specie. Should you be empowered to enter into this contract, please forward to me the particulars of said contract, and I will dispatch payment to you. Otherwise, Stephen Austin has been appointed by our government to act as minister plenipotentiary to the United States, and he will engage with his counterpart in the United States War Department to contract for these arms.

Yours Respectfully,

William B. Travis

Brigadier General Commanding Army of the Republic of Texas,

Alamo, San Antonio, Bexar, Texas

25th May 1836

The previous month had been busy for Will as he integrated the men Houston had brought with him from Columbus, after the declaration of independence was signed, as well as volunteers recently arrived from the United States. One of the men who arrived with the volunteers was a West Point graduate by the name of Albert Sidney Johnston.

As a history buff, Will recalled from his own memories, in a world now gone forever, Johnston would eventually rise to command the Texian army and a quarter century later was one of the Confederacy's leading generals. It didn't take long for Will to promote him to the rank of Lt. Colonel, placing him in command of the regular infantry battalion.

The month of May was mostly gone, and San Antonio had returned to normal, after the delegates had completed the constitution and returned home and Burnet transferred the provisional government back to Harrisburg, on Buffalo Bayou, near Galveston Bay, awaiting the plebiscite scheduled for the summer, when all Texas would vote on the constitution.

The window in Will's office was open and he and Johnston sat at the large, heavy desk, looking at a dozen military-style jackets which Will had previously ordered from New Orleans. The jackets were dyed assorted colors, ranging from the navy-blue common with the US Army, to the gray of state militia regiments in the US, and several shades in between. Will was torn between a deep-green jacket that reminded him a bit of the British Rifle uniform from the Sharpe's Rifles book and TV series and a khaki jacket that Johnston referred to as 'butternut'. The butternut jacket reminded him of a cross between a Confederate jacket and the khaki jacket used by the British at the end of the nineteenth century.

"Sid, I believe I prefer either the green or the, ah, butternut jacket, as being the best suited for wear on the frontier. What are your thoughts?" Will held both jackets up for Johnston to see.

Johnston took the butternut jacket and walked over to the adobe wall and held it up to the wall. The jacket's color blended well against the wall's dull brown. Holding the jacket there, he replied, "She's not what I would call pretty, General, but she'd serve us far better against the Comanche than any of the other colors we've been looking at. That, and look at how durable this jean material is." Johnston pulled at the seams and tried stretching the material, but the wool and cotton blended jacket took the abuse he dealt.

Will took the jacket back from Johnston and said, "Very well. Have our regimental quartermaster place a request for bids with suppliers in New Orleans. Make sure they have the specifications and that we get no less than three bids. Getting the money to pay for them may be unlikely until after presidential elections are held later this year. But it doesn't hurt to ask."

As Will left the office, he donned his blue jacket and followed Johnston down the stairs, across the plaza and through the unfinished north wall, to where a company of Johnston's infantry were practicing Will's latest skirmish tactics. They watched a team of four men advance across the prairie, as the soldier in the lead fired his rifle, he fell back to the second position while the last man in the team stepped to the front and fired. Until he could buy better equipment, this leapfrog tactic was the best option he and Johnston had designed, to combat the Comanche.

Beyond the drilling infantry, Will saw a small dust cloud making its way southward, toward the company. As it approached, the swirling dust cloud materialized into a horseman, riding hell-bent-for-leather toward the fort. A bareheaded man dressed in a tattered hunting jacket saw the two officers standing before the scaffolding of the north wall and raced his horse toward them. As he jerked the reins the horse, heavily lathered from the brutal ride, slid to a stop. The rider cried out, "The Comanches! They've killed all the men and kidnapped the women and children!"

Stay tuned for the continued adventures of the Lone Star Reloaded Series, book 2 in the Q4 of 2017.

Thank you for reading

If you enjoyed reading Forget the Alamo! Please help support the author by leaving a review where you purchased the book. For announcements, promotions, special offers, you can sign up for updates from Drew McGunn at: https://drewmcgunn.wixsite.com/website

About the Author

Drew McGunn lives in Texas with his wonderfully supportive wife. He started writing in high school and after college worked the nine-to-five grind for many years, while the stories in his head rattled around, begging to be released.

After one too many video games, Drew awoke from his desire for one more turn, and returned to his love of the printed word. His love of history led him to study his roots, and as a sixth generation Texan, he decided to write about the founding of Texas as a Republic. There were many terrific books about early Texas, but hardly any about alternate histories of the great state. With that in mind, he wrote his debut novel "Forget the Alamo!" as a reimagining of the first days of the Republic.

When he's not writing or otherwise putting food on the table, Drew enjoys traveling to historic places, or reading other engaging novels from up and coming authors.

Printed in Great Britain
by Amazon

84035283R00128